She squealed with laughter, dipping to gather more snow.

But before she could straighten again he was in front of her, pummeling her with snow. She gasped and inhaled a mouthful of sparkling wet crystals. Unable to breathe, she squealed, "Stop!"

He laughed. "I told you not to start something you couldn't finish."

But, rather than concede defeat, she used his pause to bend again, scoop up a handful of snow and toss it directly into his face.

His expression was so incredulous that Elise roared with laughter.

"Oh, this is war now."

Before she could bob down to gather more snow, Jared plowed toward her, catching her around the waist. He hit her with enough force that she lost her balance, and they both tumbled to the ground.

She managed one squeak on the way down, but when they landed with a thump—her in the blanket of soft white snow, him on top of her—her laughter stopped. The world around them hushed. The only sound was the rasp of their breathing.

Dear Reader

Every year after my son hauls the Christmas decorations into the living room, I look at the pitiful assortment and announce that next year we're starting earlier and having a better tree.

Then I proceed to hang the toilet paper roll my daughter decorated with green paint, glitter and tinsel in pre-kindergarten in the middle, where everyone can see it.

I hang the ornament with the picture of my son when he was about seven. I hang the fancy silk and lace ornament with pearl hatpin accents my friend made me, and the light-up star that hasn't worked in years, but which we bought on Christmas Eve in a year when we had very little money.

This year, though, I realised I wasn't simply hanging ornaments. I was reviewing Christmases past. Seeing memories. Seeing my kids smaller and my husband younger…and myself scrambling to pull everything together so Christmas would be perfect.

I've got friends with Victorian trees so beautiful they've stolen my breath. Friends with houses decorated to rival Trump Towers. This year I finally realised I'll always have a tree with old toilet paper rolls and pictures pasted onto ornaments by loving little hands.

May your days be merry and bright…and may all your Christmases be filled with toilet paper rolls, icing-painted cookies and memories that warm your heart.

Susan

HER BABY'S
FIRST CHRISTMAS

BY
SUSAN MEIER

MILLS & BOON®
Pure reading pleasure™

First published in Great Britain 2008
Harlequin Mills & Boon Limited,
Eton House, 18-24 Paradise Road, Richmond, Surrey TW9 1SR

© Linda Susan Meier 2008

ISBN: 978 0 263 20379 0

Set in Times Roman 10¾ on 12¾ pt
07-1008-45817

Printed and bound in Great Britain
by Antony Rowe Ltd, Chippenham, Wiltshire

Susan Meier spent most of her twenties thinking she was a job-hopper—until she began to write and realised everything that came before was only research! One of eleven children, with twenty-four nieces and nephews and three kids of her own, Susan has had plenty of real-life experience watching romance blossom in unexpected ways. She lives in Western Pennsylvania with her wonderful husband, Mike, three children, and two over-fed, well-cuddled cats, Sophie and Fluffy. You can visit Susan's website at www.susanmeier.com

CHAPTER ONE

JARED JOHNSON drove his black SUV out of the basement parking garage of Clover Valley Luxury Apartments onto the street and saw Elise McDermott standing on the corner in the pouring rain. Suitcase, diaper bag and small boxlike container on the sidewalk beside her feet, she held her baby in a carrier, which she protectively sheltered with her umbrella.

But the storm was relentless and Jared suspected it wouldn't take more than a minute or two before Elise and her baby would be soaking wet. Angry with her for standing in the rain with a baby, when she could be in their building lobby, he stopped his SUV and hit the button that lowered the passenger side window.

Leaning across his seat, he yelled, "What the hell are you doing out in this storm with a baby!"

"I'm waiting for a taxi to take me to the bus station."

With the window down he could hear the heavy California rain as it pounded his windshield, roof and hood. Obviously thinking he'd yelled to be heard over the noise and not out of anger, she stepped closer. Her pretty green eyes were dull with worry. Her thick, curly red hair danced around her in the wind.

"But I've been waiting a while. And the schedule I have has the bus leaving in a little over an hour. If I miss it I won't get to North Carolina in time to do everything I need to do before Christmas. Do you think my taxi forgot me?"

"Yes!" Guilt stabbed him. She wasn't standing in the rain like a ninny with no place to go. It sounded as if she was on her way home for the holiday. To her real home. Not a condo she was house-sitting as she'd been for the past six months for Michael Feeney while he was in Europe. And her taxi had forgotten her. She wasn't a scatterbrain. He had to stop jumping to the conclusion that everybody who did anything out of the realm of what he considered normal was somehow wrong.

Annoyed with himself, he sighed and glanced at his watch before he shoved his gearshift into Park. He was way too early for his flight anyway.

He jumped out of his SUV and rounded the hood. He knew from experience there was only one way to deal with his guilt. Penance.

"How about if I give you a ride to the bus station?"

Elise McDermott stared at dark-haired, gray-eyed, absolutely gorgeous Jared Johnson. He wore an expensive raincoat over a dark suit, white shirt and tie, and was currently getting drenched because he didn't have an umbrella. When she agreed to house-sit for Michael Feeney, Michael had told her Jared was the person to call if anything happened while he was away. He'd laughingly said Jared was grouchy but once he got over being disturbed, he would always come through, if only out of guilt. Jared had probably offered her a ride because he'd felt bad about yelling at her.

"I'd love a ride, but you're obviously on your way somewhere and I don't want to be any trouble."

He reached for her suitcase. "No trouble."

She put her hand over his on the handle. "I'm serious. You were going somewhere and I don't like to be a bother." He might want to make up for yelling at her, but he didn't have to. Being alone and pregnant she'd learned to stand on her own two feet. She didn't need to be coddled. "I'll call another cab."

"I'm on my way to the airport. But I'm early. Way too early. You'll be doing me a favor if you let me make the side trip to the bus station. I won't have to sit in the airport lounge for three hours."

"But—"

Before she could argue any further, he pulled on the suitcase, easily wrestling it away from her. "Come on."

She opened her mouth to stop him, but the wind caught her umbrella and she couldn't hold it. The rush of air jerked the handle out of her grip and it took off like a kite.

He nodded at the baby seat. "You buckle her in," he said, shouting over the noise of the storm as he began walking to the rear of the SUV. "I'll put these in the back."

She shook her head. Lord, he was persistent—and she was getting drenched. Since he was offering to do what she'd have to pay a cab to do, she supposed she'd be foolish to argue.

By the time he had her gear stowed, she was almost done with the baby. She clicked the final strap, shut the back door and settled into the passenger seat of his SUV. He slid behind the steering wheel and closed the door. Suddenly it was blessedly dry and quiet.

He hit the buttons to activate the heater and she glanced at all bells and whistles in his obviously expensive vehicle. "Wow. It's so quiet in here."

"That's one of the car's selling points. It's quiet."

"Yeah, quiet and…wonderful. Holy cow. This must have cost a chunk of change."

"It's nothing compared to the things my clients drive."

"It might be nothing compared to your clients' rides—" According to the building rumor mill, the guy in the penthouse—as Jared was known to most of the residents—was the attorney for several recording artists, one recording studio and a few movie stars, so she didn't doubt his clients drove incredibly fancy cars. "But compared to the rest of us, you're sitting pretty."

Her praise seemed to make him uncomfortable and he shifted on his seat. His jaw tightened. "I wasn't always well-off."

Because she didn't know him, had only seen him a few times in the lobby waiting for the elevator to his penthouse, she had no idea why he'd be upset to have money. But since she'd never see him again, it didn't matter. He was who he was. Rich. She was who she was—a single mom without an extra cent to spare. Six years ago when her mother died she'd left North Carolina with her boyfriend Patrick with big dreams, but she'd ended up supporting him. When she'd gotten pregnant he'd left as if his feet were on fire. She and Jared Johnson had nothing in common and there was no sense pretending they did by making mindless small talk.

She settled into the bucket seat and closed her eyes. Besides, she had a few things to think about. She was returning to North Carolina, but not the small town she grew up in. She'd inherited her grandmother's house in the town right beside it. She was going to the hometown of her father. The guy who had left her mom. The guy she didn't even know. And she wasn't sure whether the good people of Four Corners, North Carolina, would welcome her with open arms, or treat her like the plague. She only knew the grandmother she'd never met had left her a piece of property. A place she could sell, hopefully for enough money to buy a home to raise her baby.

The same grandmother who hadn't even wanted to meet her, hadn't acknowledged her as her kin, had given her her first break in life.

And she'd be a fool not to take it.

Suddenly the SUV was so quiet Jared could hear his own breathing. This was a bad idea. Elise was virtually a stranger and here they were, trapped in a car for at least twenty minutes, with nothing to talk about. He fixed his eyes on the road, occasionally glancing at the shops lining the street, then he saw the Christmas tree in front of Meg's Memory Mart, growing in a pot big enough to accommodate a four-foot fir, covered in blinking lights and tinsel. His heart caught. His breath shivered.

Stop.

She's gone.

He shifted on the seat, struggling to rein in a flood of memories. He had to get a hold of himself now, before his plane landed in New York. If he didn't, his pain would be infinitely worse when he got to the city where every damned thing on every damned street would remind him of the absolutely perfect life he'd lost. He couldn't cancel his trip. After five years of his finding excuses not to come home, his parents had threatened to come to California with their friend "the shrink" if he backed out this year. They didn't think it was natural for him to stay away as long as he had. They thought he was just a little bit crazy. He had to show them he was okay.

Even if he wasn't a hundred percent sure he was.

Blocking that last thought, he fixed his mind on upcoming contract negotiations for one of his clients, and the rest of the drive to the bus station passed in silence. He pulled up to the curb and Elise eagerly jumped out when he stopped the car. He climbed out of his side of the vehicle and headed for the back of the SUV.

"Here," he said, grabbing her suitcase before she could. "I'll get these. You get the baby."

"That's okay. I can handle it."

"I'm sure you can. But I've got plenty of time. Think of this as part of the way I'm wasting those three hours before my flight."

She rolled her eyes but strode to the side of his vehicle, letting him unload her things. He added her six-pack-size cooler and diaper bag to the suitcase he already had, and walked to the passenger's side of the SUV where she was getting her baby from the backseat.

She arranged the baby carrier in her right hand and motioned for him to slide the straps for the diaper bag and cooler to her shoulder. "I'll take those."

She wasn't going to let him help her into the bus

station? That was ridiculous. She could barely carry all these things.

Still, rather than argue, he said, "Okay," and slid the bag and cooler in place before setting the suitcase at her feet for her to take. Then he surprised her by removing the baby carrier handle from her right hand. "I'll take the baby."

"We're fine."

"I'm sure you are, but I'm happy to hold her while you get your tickets."

"I'm—"

"I know. Fine. But I have time and I can use it to save you the trouble of juggling the baby while you buy your bus tickets."

"You know, you wouldn't have to pay penance for the guilt you feel when you yell at people if you'd simply stop yelling at people."

It surprised him that she caught on to the guilt and penance thing he had going and that unexpectedly struck him as funny. Despite himself, he smiled. "Why do you think I usually just don't talk to people?"

"I thought you were a snob."

That made him out-and-out laugh. She gave him a strange look, but turned away and marched into the bus station. He followed, glancing down at the baby in the carrier. "Hey, Molly."

The chubby, curly-haired baby grinned at him, her toothless gums exposed, spit bubbles forming at the corner of her mouth. With her pale red hair, she looked adorable in her little pink one-piece outfit, bundled in blankets.

He strode to a bench seat, pleased Molly wasn't giving

him any trouble. But when Elise got in line, the baby began to fuss and then to cry. Two people took places behind Elise, putting her out of reach for assistance.

Cursing, he sat and began unbuckling the straps confining the unhappy baby. Passengers on the other benches around him turned and gave him pointed looks, letting him know how little they appreciated a crying baby in their midst.

"Hush, now. I'm going as fast as I can."

The last snap popped and he pulled Molly from her seat. She immediately stopped crying and grinned toothlessly at him.

"Oh, I get it. You did that on purpose, didn't you? Made me think you were going to make a scene when you only wanted me to pick you up?"

She cooed and her grin widened.

"Stop being cute. I'm immune."

His stern voice caused her face to pucker as if she were about to cry again and, not wanting to risk the wrath of the waiting passengers, Jared rose to walk with her.

Pacing back and forth seemed to amuse her enough that she looked around curiously. Jared relaxed. Knowing he had to keep moving, he meandered to the large screen that displayed the schedules. He scanned until he saw the one for North Carolina and his mouth fell open.

Eight days?

It would take Elise eight days to get to North Carolina? He glanced at the people milling around the bus station. Eight days on a moving vehicle with the people currently giving him beady-eyed stares, obviously not at all pleased to see that they'd be traveling with a baby? Oh, Lord. Elise was in trouble.

He glanced at the screen again to be sure he'd seen correctly and he had. Eight long days to get to North Carolina. The bus had to be taking routes that would allow it to drop other passengers along the way. Driving himself, he'd traveled from New York City to Los Angeles in five days.

He frowned. He *had* driven it in five days. If he were to drive Elise, that would cut her trip nearly in half and get her out of the bus filled with passengers who didn't want her. On top of that, those five days of driving would delay *his* arrival. He wouldn't have to spend three weeks in a city that only reminded him of what he lost. He'd have a delay in seeing, hearing, smelling things in New York that would remind him of better days. Perfect days. The perfect life that slipped through his fingers. And then he could cut another five days off because he'd have to drive back to L.A.

He shook his head in bemusement. As good as that sounded, it was a bad idea. Not only was Elise going to North Carolina, hundreds of miles south of New York City, but how would he explain it to his parents? Out of the blue he'd decided to drive a neighbor the whole way to North Carolina for the holidays? Then for sure they'd think he was insane.

He watched Elise step out of the line, holding her ticket and for a second he envied her. Relief showed on her face, but of course, that mood wouldn't last. Once the busload of passengers got fed up with her and her baby, she'd be miserable.

But he couldn't simply offer her a ride. Even if they agreed to find a bus station for her in whatever city their paths separated, he still had to have a reason for driving instead of flying—one that didn't sound like an obvious stall tactic to his parents.

Elise walked up to him and opened her arms for her baby. "What happened?"

"She cried."

"Ah, she bullied you into picking her up."

"That's exactly what it felt like."

"Well, your time of duty is up." She smiled at him. "I'm sorry if I was a bit brusque before. I'm nervous about this trip."

He glanced at his feet. "It's all right." He raised his gaze to meet hers. "I'm nervous about my trip, too."

"So we have a little in common after all."

"Yeah. That and Michael Feeney."

"Michael's been a good friend to me."

Jared nodded. "Me, too." He smiled at her, glad to have assuaged her worry over her missing the taxi by driving her to the bus station. "Have a nice trip."

"And you have a safe flight."

Jared nodded and turned to go at the same time that the loudspeaker crackled to life. "Ladies and gentle-men, we regret to inform you that trip number—"

The loudspeaker squeaked and crackled and Jared didn't hear the number, but it didn't matter. He headed for the wide, double-door entrance.

"—Final destination Raleigh, North Carolina, has been postponed due to mechanical difficulties and has been rescheduled for tomorrow at ten."

Elise glanced down at her ticket, then squeezed her eyes shut. For heaven's sake! Inheriting her grand-mother's house was supposed to be her lucky break.

Yet everything that could go wrong with this trip was going wrong. What was she supposed to do for twenty-four hours in a bus station with a baby? Maybe she could get a ticket for the next bus?

She had the idea at the same time as everybody else in the bus station. Package-laden passengers jammed the ticket window.

She stared at them in dismay, until someone grabbed her arm and turned her around.

Jared.

He let go of her arm and rammed his fingers through his thick black hair. His gray eyes circled the complex as if the last thing he wanted to do was look at her. But eventually his gaze swung around, caught hers and held it.

"Is that your bus?"

"Yes, but don't worry about it. I'll call a cab and go to a hotel. Michael's home. So I can't go back to his condo. But Molly and I will be fine."

"Not really." He turned her to face the line of passengers mobbing the ticket window. "When your baby cried, those three women over there gave me dirty looks." He turned her slightly to the right. "See that guy in the gray topcoat who looks like he has vodka for breakfast? When Molly fussed, he slammed his newspaper on the bench. They don't want to be riding with a kid who is most likely going to cry at least part of the way."

As Jared spoke, the noise and bustle of the bus terminal pressed in on Elise. She expected the trip to be long and boring. She even anticipated that people would get restless, maybe even edgy, but she hadn't factored in their reactions to a fussy baby. She was about to spend eight days on a bus with a six-month-old who would probably cry most of the way. Forget about her own misery. It would be eight days in hell for everybody who rode with them.

She faced Jared again. "Why do you care?"

"I was thinking that maybe we should ride together."

"You're flying."

"I *was* flying. Looking at the schedule over there, I decided that I want to drive instead."

"Right. You want the trip to take a week instead of a few hours."

"Actually I do." He combed his fingers through his hair again. "Look, I'll take you as far as I can until you have to head south, then I'll help you find a bus station."

The deal sounded like a good one, but it had also sounded perfectly logical when Patrick told her he was going upstate to look for work after she told him she was pregnant. Michael was the only person she'd dared to trust in months, and that trust had been hard won. She might have made the mistake of trusting Patrick too easily, but she wouldn't do it again.

"No, thanks. I'm fine."

He drew an annoyed breath. "Look, I don't want to spend four weeks in New York with my parents badgering me about my life. Reading that schedule I figured out that I could shave ten days off my trip if I drove."

She sighed. "Either your life is more pathetic than mine, or that's a lame excuse to hide the fact that you feel sorry for me."

He laughed. "Honey, if you think I feel sorry for you, then you don't know me very well. I only do good deeds as penance. And right now I don't have anything to make up to you. I did my good deeds for the time I yelled."

Elise thought about that for a second, and then she smiled. "Your life *is* more pathetic than mine." She shook her head. "You want to drive home, but you can't just *decide* to drive. You need an excuse for your parents."

He gave her a blank look. "Didn't I just say that?"

"Sort of, but not really." She laughed. "Molly and I are your excuse. You're going to tell your parents that you're driving a new mom and her baby home because their bus was canceled and they're not going to question that."

Again, he said nothing. But he didn't have to. His bland expression confirmed her suspicion.

Elise glanced around the noisy bus station. Facing a day's wait and not wanting to spend money on a hotel room, Elise was more than tempted to accept his offer.

She turned to him again. "How do I know I can trust you?"

"Trust me?"

"Yeah, how do I know you're not going to leave me along the side of the road or something?"

"Why would I do that when you already figured out that I need you?"

She sighed in exasperation. "Because my mother warned me about getting into cars with strangers."

"I'm not a stranger. We've seen each other at least once a week waiting for the elevator."

"Yeah, and we've never spoken."

"Fine. If you're concerned, call Michael. He'll vouch for me. Besides—" He glanced at the baby in her arms, but quickly brought his gaze back to Elise's.

"I don't date, fool around with or even talk to women with kids. Even if I did, you're not my type. You're short. And puny. I like my women with a little meat on their bones."

He looked at her again. His eyes made a quick journey across her face and down her slender torso. "You're not my type."

The man was so honest Elise wasn't sure if she should be insulted or laugh. She glanced at Molly, who was calm in her arms, but who wouldn't be so happy on a bus for eight days, then at dark-haired Jared, with his gorgeous face made of sharp angles and planes and eyes the color of the sky right before a storm. She might think he was one of the most handsome men in the world, but as he'd said, she wasn't his type. Plus, Michael had told her that if she was ever in trouble, Jared was the guy to call. Though having a bus trip postponed wasn't exactly trouble, if he was offering a ride, she'd be a fool not to take it.

"Give me five minutes to call Michael."

"Take your time. The longer your call, the longer my delay."

CHAPTER TWO

"MICHAEL says you're as trustworthy as the three wise men."

"Great. Let's go." Jared grabbed her suitcase, cooler and diaper bag and led her to the bench where he'd left the baby carrier. She laid Molly inside, but he didn't even pause. He walked outside without her. She finished settling Molly, exited the bus terminal and saw him standing at the SUV, stashing her belongings in the rear compartment.

At his car, she opened the back door to install the baby carrier and Jared was suddenly at her side. "Here, let me."

He reached for the seat belt at the same time Elise did. Their shoulders brushed then their arms, and then their fingers. A jolt of electricity sizzled through Elise. She froze, but so did Jared. He turned his head slightly to the right, catching her gaze with his serious gray eyes.

She didn't even react. Jared was a very handsome, sexy guy. Of course, she was attracted to him. But she wasn't going to do anything about it. And neither was he. She might be more "his type" than he let on, but he clearly didn't want anything to do with her. And that was much, much better for two people about to spend several days in each other's company, than giving in to a meaningless attraction.

She held his gaze blandly, as if what they'd felt meant nothing. His steely-gray eyes probed hers for another second or two then he turned away. Her breath streamed out of her lungs in a quiet swoosh of relief.

Once Molly was strapped in, Jared slammed the door, pulled open the passenger door for Elise and rounded the hood. As he slid behind the steering wheel, Elise buckled her seat belt. He started the car, and without a word they began their trip.

It didn't take long to get onto a highway. California was riddled with them. But when he turned onto Route 5 north, Elise frowned.

"Why aren't we going east?"

"Five takes us to Route 80, which will take me the entire way to New York City. If I'm remembering correctly you can ride with me as far as Pennsylvania and get a bus south."

"Okay." She didn't know a lot about the road systems, but it seemed he did. "Sounds great."

With the directions out of the way and Molly happily occupied in the backseat, the only sound in the SUV was the faint *thwap* of the windshield wipers. Jared shifted on his seat as if as uneasy as she was. But she didn't think he was antsy because of the silence. A man who never even said hello while standing with her waiting for the elevator was probably more afraid that she *would* talk than she wouldn't. So she said nothing, respecting his right to keep to himself.

They drove about twenty miles before the rain slowed to a drizzle. Jared flicked a switch and the low *thwap, thwap, thwap* of the wiper blades slowed, too, making the quiet in the car even more pronounced. Molly woke the second the sound changed, as if the comforting rhythm had soothed her and, without it, she couldn't sleep.

Hearing her stir, Elise twisted on the seat to face her daughter. Though Molly was lying facing the back of the SUV, a mirror not only caught her reflection, but it also caught Elise's for the baby. Molly glanced around as if disoriented, then screamed like a banshee.

"Hey, Molly. Hey, baby," Elise crooned. "See. Your mama's here. There's no reason to cry."

Molly stretched out her little arms to Elise's reflection in the mirror, her cries echoing through the vehicle.

"We're going to have to stop to feed her."

"Stop?"

"Just pull to the side of the road. It only takes her five minutes to eat."

He sighed. "Right." But he pulled off the road.

He pulled off the road and, not wanting to annoy him or waste any time, she raced to the back of the SUV, got a bottle from the cooler, retrieved Molly from the car seat and quickly fed her, then burped her. Normally she would have spent a few extra minutes playing with her and talking to her, but wanting to keep the peace, she put Molly back into her seat, stowed the bottle in the little cooler and returned to the passenger side.

Jared immediately got them back on the road. "So how often does she need feeding?"

Elise winced. "Every three or four hours."

"Do I have to watch the clock?"

Elise laughed. "No. Molly will remind us when she's hungry."

Jared didn't reply. The song that had been playing softly in the background from the radio he'd turned on while she fed Molly suddenly became static as if they'd driven out of range of the station.

"I'll find another channel."

"Great."

Elise set the dial for a country station, but rather than the twang of a country song, the joyful strains of Christmas carols filled the car. Jared reached down, pressed a button and soft rock poured from the speakers.

No surprise there. She'd already figured out he didn't like Christmas.

He had lots of money but wasn't happy, and he didn't want to go home for Christmas but he had to. There was so much more to this man than met the eye, but Elise had no intention of probing. She had her own troubles to deal with. Getting to North Carolina three days sooner meant she'd get to Four Corners three days sooner. And she had no idea what kind of reception she'd get.

Had her grandmother ever mentioned her to people? Did anyone even know she existed? And why did her grandmother leave her the house when her father should have been the one to inherit it?

For all she knew her father could have had a falling out with his mother and she could be walking into the aftermath of that. Plus, he could have other children. She could have half brothers and sisters. Some might even live in Four Corners. Once they heard who inherited their grandmother's property, they might also be angry about her being the one to get the farm.

Of course, they might welcome her into the family.

She squeezed her eyes shut. Hoping for that was just wrong. Not because it wasn't in the realm of possibility, but because if she let herself believe it, she could end up hurt. And she'd had enough hurt in her life. Her dad had left. Her mom had died the summer after Elise graduated from high school. Patrick hadn't wanted her. Or their baby.

So, no. She couldn't handle any more disappointment and she wouldn't hope for things that were at best wishful thinking.

She drew a breath, tried to shake off the fantasy that she might have family who wanted her, but it wouldn't go away. She saw holiday celebrations in her head, gifts to buy and get from people who loved her, and maybe even Christmas morning at a home filled with love and laughter.

Of course, she could also spend Christmas morning listening to somebody scream at her that she didn't deserve their grandmother's land.

Hating her thoughts, she squelched a sigh. She'd managed not to think about any of this for the past month. But the silent car provided too much opportunity for her mind to feed her fears *and* her fantasies.

"How long do you think this trip will take?"

Jared flexed his hands on the steering wheel. "If I drive fast it's four days. Normal speed it's five."

Four or five days until she faced her future. Maybe even her father. Maybe even a family.

Her stomach quaked. It seemed too soon. Yet four days was also a bit too long to sit in a silent car bouncing between fear and wishes.

* * *

At noon, Jared's stomach growled and he took an exit ramp off the highway, suggesting they eat lunch. They ate an uneventful hamburger and fries in a fast food restaurant, and then got back on the road. Molly fell asleep almost instantly and Jared let the country music channel Elise had found fill the silent air.

At six o'clock, stiff from driving, he turned to Elise. "What do you say we stop for the night?"

She glanced up at the highway sign. "This is it? This is all the farther we're going? We're not even out of Nevada."

Ignoring her protest, he said, "Watch the road signs. We'll take the exit with the first hotel."

"But it's only six o'clock."

"And my back is stiff."

"I can drive."

He peered at her. "Are you kidding? Do you think I'd give you my keys so you could forget to give them back and then drive away in the middle of the night with my SUV?"

She sighed. "You can't be that distrustful."

He turned his attention to the road again. "I know you're eager to get home so I promise we'll make better time tomorrow."

She said, "Okay," but Jared heard something odd in her voice and decided it was disappointment. Though he tried not to, he remembered times he had been eager to get home. He drew a breath, banishing the memories of homemade cookies sprinkled with sugar that MacKenzie had dyed red and green to make it more festive. Of welcome home kisses at the apartment door.

Of cuddling together to stay warm in bed because the superintendent turned down the heat at night.

"There. Look." Elise's voice brought him out of his thoughts. "There's a hotel just off this exit."

He maneuvered the big SUV down the ramp. When they reached the hotel, he drove under the portico, shut off his engine and jumped out of the car. Elise climbed out, too. She immediately opened the back door and freed Molly.

"Hey, kid," Jared said as Elise walked up to him.

Molly sniffed and snuggled into her mother's shoulder.

"She's not quite awake enough to remember you," Elise explained.

"I'm not offended."

Jared made his reservation first, so he could take both Molly and the diaper bag from Elise. She opened her purse and pulled out a wallet and though Jared wasn't one to be nosy, he couldn't help noticing that she didn't seem to have a lot of cash. Telling himself she probably had a bank card and a few large bills, rather than several smaller bills, he walked away, cooing to Molly who sniffled as if she wanted to cry.

"How much is it for a night… exactly?"

Hearing Elise's question, Jared paced a bit farther away from the hotel desk. He remembered that same tone in Mackenzie's voice when she asked the superintendent how much the rent was for their first apartment. Jared had been about to ask, but she beat him to it. She fancied herself their money manager. The memory of how bad she was with finances made him laugh, and then pinched his chest with wrenching pain.

He immediately pushed those thoughts aside, diverting his attention to Elise for the distraction. But remembering how embarrassing it was to need to know to the exact penny how much something cost, he took a few more steps away. Even then he heard her asking for the cheapest room and groaning when the desk clerk told her that all the rooms were priced the same. A price that was obviously too high for her.

Jared wanted to kick himself for not considering cost when he chose a place to stop for the night, but he also couldn't go over and tell her that they could drive some more until they found a less expensive place. That would only embarrass her more. He considered paying for her hotel room, but knew she wouldn't accept that, either. The woman was a walking pillar of pride. She clearly didn't like taking help.

But her situation reminded him so much of himself and MacKenzie at the beginning of their marriage that he couldn't simply ignore her. He hadn't minded doing without, but he'd hated that MacKenzie had spent the last years of her life gazing longingly through storefront windows at things she couldn't have. And Elise was a new mom. No new mom should be broke. If Jared knew the name of the man who had deserted her with a baby, he'd kick the guy's behind.

But he couldn't. He didn't even know if the guy had left Elise or if it had been her decision not to tell her baby's father she was pregnant. For all he knew, Elise might have never even told Molly's dad he was a father. She was an independent thing—

He stopped his thoughts. None of this was any of his business.

Key card in hand, she approached him with a smile, pretending everything was fine. "All set."

He pretended, too. "All set."

She reached for Molly, but he said, "I'm okay with Molly. We'll get you settled in your room first, and then I'll take my stuff to my room and park the car."

At the SUV he gave her the baby so he could take her suitcase, diaper bag and cooler. "What's in this?"

"Her milk, some juice, some baby cereal. I have crackers and cookies in my suitcase for me. So if you get hungry or feel like a cookie, I have some."

He again thought of MacKenzie's red and green sugar-covered cookies and the deep breath he took shivered in his lungs. But his voice was calm when he said, "I'm not much of a cookie guy anymore."

"Okay. But just in case."

Knowing she needed the assurance that he didn't think himself too good for her things, he nodded, and then followed her to her room, watching as she inserted the key and opened the door all without causing Molly to stir.

She walked in, looking around as if she'd never seen a hotel room before. "Wow! This is a great room."

He glanced at the room. At best it was adequate.

"I can see why it cost so much."

And the price, while not low, certainly wasn't high.

But—as he'd already reminded himself—Elise and her finances were none of his business. He handed Molly to Elise and headed for the door. "Good night."

"Good night, Jared."

But when he reached the door, she said, "And Jared?"

He paused, facing her again.

"Thanks. I know you're delaying your trip to New

York for your own reasons, but giving us a ride saved me a lot of headaches. I really appreciate it."

Something inside Jared stirred. It wasn't the first time anyone had thanked him in the past five years, but this was the first time being thanked had made him feel good. He'd fallen so far into a black pit of despair that work had become his only motivation to get up some mornings. He would lose himself in the sometimes ridiculous trials and tribulations of his wealthy clients so he didn't have to deal with his own life. He'd forgotten how good it felt to help someone.

MacKenzie would be so ashamed of him.

Some days he was ashamed of himself. But he supposed that was what happened when life threw a man a curve like the one thrown to him. He hadn't lost his ability to function. He'd lost his ability to feel. Or maybe he'd lost his humanity. Yet, here it was, staring him in the face. And for the first time in five years, being himself didn't hurt.

"You're welcome."

Elise was already at breakfast when Jared arrived in the lobby the next morning. His gray raincoat, creased trousers and dress shirt of the day before had been replaced by jeans, a T-shirt and a leather jacket. He looked younger and more relaxed. So handsome she wasn't surprised when the hotel desk clerk gave him a quick once-over or that her own heart stuttered in her chest at the mere sight of him.

As he approached the little table where she and Molly sat sharing a bowl of hot cereal, her nerves tingled with the attraction she'd felt the day before when they'd accidentally brushed hands. She once again reminded herself that being attracted wasn't in either of their best interest but this time it didn't work. How could she not be attracted to him? Incredibly male in his jeans and leather jacket, he took her breath away. If they accidentally touched again, she knew she'd shiver.

Still, she didn't let any of that show as she offered him the empty seat at her small table. To her surprise, he not only took it; he actually made baby talk with Molly as he ate. Luckily, when they got into the SUV, he didn't talk anymore, except to suggest they stop for lunch when Molly awakened after sleeping away the morning.

Back in the car after their quick lunch, he once again stayed silent until Molly awakened from her afternoon nap and they stopped for dinner.

They traveled another two hours after supper. Then it began to rain again and Jared suggested Elise look for a hotel. She found one almost immediately, but when she wrapped fingers around the handle to open her door, Jared grabbed her forearm.

"Before we go in, let's have a chat."

The unexpected touch of his fingers on her skin sizzled through her. Then his serious tone penetrated, and the heat evaporated.

"Chat" was the word her mom had used when she sat Elise down to explain that her father had left them. When Elise finally found Patrick after he hadn't come home from his supposed job search, he had also said it was time for a chat. His "chat" revolved around the fact that he hadn't loved her for some time and included his complete horror at becoming a daddy.

Then he'd kicked her out of the apartment of his new girlfriend and in what felt like seconds she was suddenly on her own. Alone and pregnant.

"Chatting" never worked out well for her.

"Why do we need to chat?"

He drew a long breath. "I know you don't have a lot of money and I do, so why don't we let this trip be totally on me?"

Relief flooded her that he wasn't angry, but when she realized what he was asking, her blood went cold. "I don't need your charity."

"I know that. But I'd like you to think of me paying for the hotel room as something like a Christmas gift."

She laughed. "You wouldn't have bought me a Christmas gift if we were still back at Clover Valley. So, no."

"Why won't you just accept my help?"

"Because I don't need it." Because she didn't want to become indebted, or worse dependent. Any time she relied on anyone, especially a man, he let her down. She didn't want to add another name to the list.

"Michael paid me very well to house-sit. For the past six months I didn't have rent or utilities. So I saved most of that money. Just because I'm frugal doesn't mean I'm broke."

She pushed out of the SUV before he could argue and immediately gasped. The air was freezing! The wind howled and the rain that pricked her felt like ice. A Southern California girl who had been raised in North Carolina, she wasn't accustomed to temperatures this low, or wind this cruel.

She scurried to the back of the SUV to gather her things, but Jared was already there.

"You grab Molly and go ahead in." He pointed at the hotel doors. "I'll be right behind you."

Elise grabbed Molly and ran into the lobby. As he had promised, Jared was right behind her, carrying her diaper bag, suitcase and cooler and his own duffel. Wind followed them inside and he had to put down the baggage to close the door.

"Wow."

"Yeah, wow," Jared agreed, but his gaze was on the line at the check-in desk. "Seems like the weather caused everybody on the road to stop. We better get a place in line before all the rooms are gone." He slid the diaper bag and her suitcase straps to her shoulders. "Take these and go sit." He nodded at the sofa and chair arranged by a fireplace. "I'll check us both in."

She caught his arm. "Don't pay for my room."

"I'll use my credit card to check you in. Then tomorrow you can pay for your room however you want."

She had expected him to argue. When he didn't, she was impressed that he respected her and her wishes. She relaxed a bit. "Okay."

"I still think you're crazy not to take my help."

"Whatever."

The first customer finished and everybody moved forward. Another clerk stepped out from a door behind the desk and called the next customer in the line. Guests were checked in quickly and soon it was Jared's turn.

Preoccupied with entertaining Molly, Elise didn't pay much attention until she heard Jared say, "Are you kidding?"

She looked over. She had a sneaking suspicion that the prices had risen sharply because of supply and demand in the storm.

She walked up to the desk. Jared said to the clerk, "Tell her what you just told me."

The young man smiled ruefully. "I'm sorry, miss, but we have only one room left."

Because that wasn't what she expected to hear, Elise blinked.

Jared sighed. "Tell her the rest."

The clerk winced. "It has only one bed."

This time, Elise's mouth fell open. "Are you kidding?"

"Tell her the other thing."

The clerk winced again. "We're the last hotel for fifty miles. That's why we booked up so quickly."

Elise stood, openmouthed, processing that. Finally she shook her head and said, "We don't have a choice."

"Looks that way."

The repentant clerk said, "Sorry."

"It's not your fault," Elise said, smiling at him, though she wanted to groan in misery. Riding in the silent car wasn't exactly torture, but it wasn't pleasant, either. She'd been looking forward to being in her own room with Molly for a few hours to simply relax. Worse, she was more attracted to Jared than she cared to admit. There'd be no downtime to remind herself that these physical feelings meant nothing. No time to remind herself that men usually spelled trouble. Especially men she depended on. And like it or not, she was depending on Jared for a ride.

One bed meant they'd either sleep together awkwardly, stiff and fearful all night that they might accidentally touch, or they'd have to flip a coin with the loser sleeping on the floor. But that wasn't the clerk's fault or Jared's.

Smiling at the clerk again, she said, "Can we have a crib for the room?"

The clerk typed a bit, probably checking availability, and then breathed a sigh of relief. "There's one left."

"One's all we need." She faced Jared again. "You get the key. I'll gather my things."

Jared nodded.

As Elise walked away, Molly cooed happily.

"Yeah. You're going to love this because you'll drink a bottle and fall asleep in a nice comfy crib that you don't have to share with a stranger. Things aren't so simple for adults."

Molly giggled. Elise rolled her eyes as she reached down for her diaper bag, suitcase and cooler. She didn't think Jared would make a pass at her or even flirt with her. He also wouldn't be so disrespectful as to come out of the bathroom wrapped only in a towel or to sleep naked. She wasn't worried that something big would happen. Little things would be the problem. Close quarters would multiply their awareness of each other and that would make the night long and uncomfortable.

Jared walked over to the seating arrangement and took the bags from her. "We're just around the corner. I'll go with you and Molly to the room, open the door and then go back and park the SUV."

He looked so nervous that Elise smiled reassuringly. "Thanks."

He motioned her to precede him out the door. Elise

stepped out into the cold again, tucking Molly's blanket tightly around her as they ran to the door of the hotel room. Jared let them in, deposited her things in the closet and left quickly.

When he was gone, Elise got a fresh bottle for Molly and sat on the bed. Spending the night in the same room was going to be too awkward for words. But right now her baby needed to be fed, so she occupied herself with feeding Molly, cooing to her as she suckled, putting her fears behind her until she actually had to face them.

When Molly was done eating, Jared opened the door. He walked his duffel bag to the closet and tossed it beside her suitcase. The intimacy of their things sitting together sent nerves thrumming through Elise. She swallowed.

"Do you and Molly need the bathroom first?"

He turned as he asked the question, and Elise's eyes made an involuntary sweep of his body. Strong thighs encased in his jeans. Tight tummy beneath a T-shirt. Broad shoulders.

A shiver of feminine longing raced through her.

Lord, why had she done that?

She redirected her gaze and her attention to Molly's diaper bag and began rifling through it for a clean diaper and pajamas. "That would be a good idea. That way I can put her to sleep while you're showering."

He frowned. "I know I'm new at this whole baby thing, but what do you do with her while *you're* showering?"

"She sits in the baby seat in the bathroom, so I can peek at her occasionally and hear her if she cries."

"Why not just bring her out here once she's had her bath and is in her pajamas?"

"I don't want to bother you."

He met her gaze. "Aren't we past that yet?"

His usually stormy-gray eyes were no less troubled tonight. If anything, they seemed to be churning with even more emotion. Or maybe a new emotion. He needed her to trust him. Their situation was awkward but they were both honest, decent people. If she didn't know at least that about him, how could he stay in the same room with her for an entire night? And if he couldn't sleep in the only room left in the hotel, where would he sleep? The SUV? The hotel lobby?

They'd been handing the baby back and forth enough already that it really did seem ridiculous to have Molly sit in the baby seat on the floor of the bathroom. Surely she could muster that much trust.

"I guess."

"So when you're done with her, bring her out and tell me what to do."

"Okay."

"Okay."

He picked up the television remote control from the dresser, and Elise took Molly, her clean clothes and her baby soaps and lotions into the bathroom. She didn't have any accessories like a baby tub, so she had to hold Molly with one hand and scrub her with the other. By the time she was done, Elise was nearly as wet as Molly.

She walked the baby into the bedroom. Jared sat on the bed, pillow propped behind him, watching the news. He met her gaze. "What do you want me to do with Molly?"

She could have happily drowned in his pretty gray eyes. But except for the fleeting attraction she'd felt from him the time they loaded her things into the SUV at the bus stop, the only emotion she'd gotten from him was his need to be trusted. The physical attraction appeared to be only her battle. And it was a stupid battle. Really. Her being worried that a rich guy who worked with celebrities wanted her so much he wouldn't be able to control himself? Now *that* was wishful thinking.

So she looked away, pretending great interest in stowing Molly's dirty clothes in the plastic bag she kept in her suitcase for laundry. "She's eaten and she's clean. So she's probably sleepy. Usually I would hold her or play with her until she rubs her eyes, then I'd put her in bed."

"Then, that's what I'll do."

"Crib's not here yet."

"It's a busy night. I'm sure it will be here by the time Molly's ready to go to sleep. If not, we'll watch TV."

She took a breath, suddenly uncomfortable. Deep down, she knew he wouldn't do anything to hurt Molly. Yet part of her shimmied with fear over leaving her with him. "I don't feel right about this."

"Afraid I'll wait until you're occupied and steal her the way I was afraid you'd steal my SUV if I left you with the keys?"

She laughed uneasily. "No. But—"

"But you don't think I'm capable of entertaining Molly?"

"I know you are."

"Then what?"

It seemed foolish to lump him in with her untrustworthy dad and equally untrustworthy Patrick, when
all Jared was asking to do was watch her baby for a
few minutes. Still, now that the moment was here it felt
wrong to simply trust him. To trust anybody.

"I just don't like anybody doing the things I'm
supposed to be doing."

"Why?"

"*Why?*"

"Yeah, why?"

She remembered being about ten, sitting by the
window of the little house she shared with her mom,
praying her dad would come back—wishing her mom
wouldn't have to worry anymore, but he never did. Not
even for a visit.

She thought of Patrick. Thought of how much easier
the first months of her pregnancy would have been if
he'd simply stuck with her. But when the going got
tough, Patrick definitely got going. It never even
occurred to him to stay with her. To help her.

Was it any wonder she didn't believe any man
would follow through?

"Just go shower. We have to be on the road early."

The faint amusement in Jared's voice brought her
back to reality. He thought she was silly to argue. He'd
been doing things like this all along. Taking the baby
while she registered in the hotel the night before or paid
restaurant checks when they stopped to eat. He didn't
understand that this time she wouldn't be a few feet
away. She'd be in another room. In a stream of water
too loud to hear what was going on with her baby in
the bedroom. And even if there was a noise loud

enough to reach her, she couldn't run out to check because she'd be naked—

Oh Lord, maybe she knew what her problem was. She didn't so much fear leaving Molly with Jared, as she feared that she'd hear a noise and she'd bolt out of the bathroom half-dressed. And it was ridiculous. Not only was Jared capable of keeping something earth-shattering from happening in the five or ten minutes she'd need to shower, but also she wouldn't come running out of the bathroom without at least grabbing a towel.

There was nothing to worry about.

After one quick glance to be sure Molly was okay, she turned and went into the bathroom.

She came out a few minutes later clean and dry, wearing sweatpants and a huge T-shirt to sleep in—the most unsexual outfit she could find in her suitcase. The crib had arrived and was set up in a corner of the room. Molly slept soundly surrounded by her familiar blankets. Jared still sat on the bed, propped on the pillow that leaned against the headboard, looking casual and comfortable and oh, so sexy.

She told herself to stop thinking that, but the very quiet, very private room with only one bed, and the intimacy of doing things like shower, seemed to multiply his sexuality. His disheveled hair and whisker-stubbled chin gave him a dark, rebellious look that spoke to everything feminine in her.

She tugged on the hem of the shirt, nervously pulling it down as far as it would go, twisting it in her hands, wishing with all her might that she would stop noticing him this way.

"Thanks for…um…taking care of Molly."

"You're welcome." He rolled off the bed and grabbed his duffel, heading for the bathroom, either blissfully unaware of her ridiculous attraction or ignoring it.

When he was behind the closed bathroom door, Elise squeezed her eyes shut. She wished she could just run away. But she couldn't. He was her driver. She wasn't even sure where they were or where she could find a bus. And how could she take Molly out in this storm? They were stuck in this room together for the night.

Worse, in a few seconds, Jared would be the one beyond the thin wall naked under the stream of water. She grabbed the remote control and found a television station. She desperately needed to divert her attention.

Jared stepped into the bathroom confused about Elise. Her very evident physical attraction to him would have made him nervous, except he knew there was no way in hell she'd ever act on it. Mostly because she didn't trust him and he sincerely doubted she ever would.

It infuriated him that after all the time they'd spent together he still had to coax her to let him watch Molly while she showered. He could believe Michael paid her well to housesit for six months. He could believe Elise saved all her money. Both of which were good reasons she could afford to pay her own expenses. So he hadn't realized just how stubborn she was until the disagreement over him watching Molly.

That had shown him something he should have paid more attention to before, but had glossed over. She wasn't simply independent about paying her own way; she didn't really like him doing *anything* for her. She was the first woman he'd met in five years who didn't see him as the source of every answer to all of her troubles. Of course, the only women he dealt with were clients, so he couldn't be too hard on them for expecting him to do his job. But having to fight Elise for the "privilege" of helping her really wore on him.

He turned on the shower, stripped and stepped under the hot spray. He was so accustomed to people depending on him that he had to reach the whole way back to his days as an assistant district attorney to remember the last time he'd met a woman this distrustful. Those were the women he'd interviewed who had been battered and abused. He wondered again about the man who had left Elise and fought back the urge to find the guy and knock him into tomorrow. It wasn't his business, but right at this moment that didn't matter. Any time he had prepared a woman to testify against an abusive man he'd fought these same urges—

He froze under the hot spray. Shampoo bubbles slid down his forehead and into his eyes. He'd just thought of the past and his chest hadn't tightened. He'd remembered being an assistant district attorney without reliving the pain.

Before he had a chance to really delve into what that meant, the shampoo stung his eyes and he shoved his head under the water. He washed himself, dried and put on the same kind of outfit Elise had. Sweatpants and a black T-shirt. If her outfit was intended to tell him she was off-limits, he'd use his to show her he got the message and agreed.

But as he squeezed paste onto his toothbrush, he suddenly realized she would fight him about who would sleep on the bed and he groaned in frustration. Everything with this woman turned into a battle.

Ready to simply tell her she was sleeping on the bed and he was sleeping on the floor, he marched out of the bathroom only to find her standing in his path, holding a coin, ready to flip it.

He stopped dead in his tracks. Her pretty red hair glistened in the light of the lamp on the dresser. Her T-shirt skimmed her breasts and hinted at the curve of her waist, the swell of her hips. The sharp, spicy scent of her shampoo mixed with remnants of the soap or shower gel she'd used and floated to his nostrils.

Reaction ricocheted through him. And again his brain sort of froze, unable to believe what was happening. He hadn't felt an actual attraction to a woman in so long that the responses rolling through him right now were foreign, novel. Yearnings and needs that had lain dormant burst to life. For the first time in five years his hormones demanded control.

But Elise was the absolutely worst woman to be awakening his sexual urges. Not just because they were traveling together, but because she reminded him of the abused women he'd prepped for trial as an assistant district attorney.

What if Elise had been abused?

She probably wouldn't have trusted him enough to ride across the country with him if she'd been physically abused. But from his two years as an A.D.A., he did know that emotional abuse could make a person antisocial. Overly independent.

Yeah. Something was definitely up with Elise and he wouldn't do anything to make it worse.

He snatched the coin from her fingers before she realized what he was doing. He tossed it in the air, caught it and set it on the back of his hand with a smack. "Heads or tails?"

"Tails."

He peered down. Saw the tails side of the coin and said, "Too bad. It's heads. I sleep on the floor." Then he tossed her coin back to her.

She caught it deftly. "Wait! I didn't see the coin."

"You have it in your hand."

"You know what I mean. I didn't see that it really was heads. You can't just bully me…"

"Bully you into sleeping on the bed?" He laughed and walked to the closet, where he extracted the extra pillow and blanket. "Wow. What a horrible man I am for giving you the bed."

"But I—"

"—Won the toss and get to sleep on the bed," he said, walking to the open space at the other side of the room where he could spread out a blanket and drop his pillow. No matter how far away he walked, he could still smell her.

Yeah, it was better for him to sleep on the floor.

CHAPTER THREE

JARED awakened to the sound of laughter. He bounced up quickly and groaned. Not only was it still dark, but sleeping on the floor had played hell with his back.

He turned and saw a small strip of light coming from the bathroom, then heard Elise say, "Oh, you like that, do you?"

Her soft, feminine voice reminded him of how much trouble he'd had falling asleep while surrounded by her scents and listening to her rustle the bed sheets as she tossed and turned.

He pulled in a breath to banish all that from his mind and called, "Everything okay in there?"

"What?"

"I said—" He stopped, hauled himself off the floor and went to the bathroom door. Though it was partially open, he turned his head, not venturing to look inside. "I asked if everything was okay in there."

"Yeah."

Elise pulled open the door. Sitting on the floor, balancing Molly on two wobbly legs, she grinned up at him. "Molly's up for a while. You might as well take the bed."

"No. That's okay, I'll—"

"No," Elise interrupted with a laugh. Her pretty red hair tumbled around her in sexy disarray. Her green eyes sparkled. "I'm serious. She's up. Maybe for the rest of the night."

He'd never seen her this relaxed before, which was probably why her femininity instantly hit him straight in the groin. It was as if her physical attractiveness and the joy she took in being a mother combined to make her incredibly womanly tonight.

"Molly's spent the past two days sleeping as we drove, so I've been expecting a night when she wouldn't sleep. Plus, she needs a little playtime. Since she sleeps all day, it doesn't matter that she's getting her playtime in the middle of the night."

He cleared his throat, unhappy that he'd been staring at her. It would be cause for celebration that he was finally finding any woman attractive again, but— as he'd already reminded himself—this particular woman had to be off-limits. She was a mom and his passenger. She was at his mercy until they got to Pennsylvania. He didn't want her to have to worry that he'd make unwanted advances. Especially since he was now concerned about her past, worried that Molly's father had abused her.

"What about you?"

She laughed. "What about me?"

Her laughter seemed to skim along his nerve endings, tempting him to smile at her, and emphasizing the intimacy of the moment. Not because they were alone in a hotel room, not even because they were talking, but because of the way they were relating. Sort of like equals…or partners…or friends.

Friends?

No. They couldn't become friends. That would make the physical attraction seem okay. And it wasn't. Seriously. She couldn't get involved with the likes of him and if they became too friendly, he'd kiss her and once he kissed her they'd cross one line after another until they were sleeping together. Being too chummy wasn't good.

His gaze rippled over her slender form. Lord, had he really told her she wasn't his type?

He took a long breath and forced his voice to be gruff when he said, "Aren't you tired?"

"Yes and no. Yes because I didn't have enough sleep. No because we've been doing nothing but sit in the SUV. I'm sure I can catch a catnap tomorrow while you're driving." She smiled again. "Please. Take the bed."

Her far-too-infrequent smile gave him a funny feeling in the pit of his stomach. It joined with all the other thoughts, feelings and yearnings that were mixing and mingling through his nervous system and bloodstream. He had to stop this. At the very least he had to get the hell away from her.

"Okay. I'll take the bed." His back nearly sang the "Hallelujah Chorus" at the thought of lying on a mattress, but his conscience pricked. How could he take a bed from a mother who obviously needed her sleep? Molly would tire out eventually and then where would Elise sleep? On the floor? That was also wrong.

He rubbed his hand along the back of his neck. "I don't feel right about this."

"Well, go and sleep on the floor then."

"You're grumpy." Thank God. "You need to get back into bed."

"I'm not grumpy." She lifted Molly from the floor and cuddled her. "I'm simply not going to coddle you. You're an adult. If you want to treat yourself poorly by playing the martyr and sleeping on the floor when I'm telling you Molly's not going to go back to bed so I can't, either, then suit yourself. You're a grown man."

Obviously she didn't realize what a huge deal it was for him to turn off the first attraction he'd felt in five years or she'd be at least a little grateful.

Insulted by her tone, he pulled away from the door. She could have taken another minute to convince him that she wouldn't be going back to bed. Instead she made the discussion about him. As if his desire to be polite and considerate of a new mother was somehow wrong. For Pete's sake, he never asked to be coddled.

Halfway to the bed, he paused. He might not ever ask to be coddled, but he did sort of like to get his own way. And maybe she had a point about the martyr thing.

He took a breath, snatched his pillow from the floor and headed for the bed, mumbling, "Whatever."

This is what happened when he let himself have emotions. From here on out he wasn't paying any attention to them.

He slid the pillows she'd used to the other side, not wanting to bury his nose in the scent she undoubtedly left behind, and dropped his own pillow below the headboard. Ripping back the covers, he yawned, and then fell onto the very comfortable bed. With a deep, relaxing breath he closed his eyes.

Elise's muffled giggle floated into the bedroom. "There you go! You're such a good girl!"

She whispered the praise, but in the quiet of the night Jared could easily hear her.

"You're not just the prettiest baby this side of the Rockies, you're also a big girl who can almost stand all by herself."

Unable to stop himself, Jared smiled. He might not want to get too friendly with Elise but Molly was a cute kid. And as far as babies went she'd been a dream through their two days on the road. How could he resist smiling about her?

"I wish I could be sure what kind of reception we're going to get in Four Corners."

Elise had dropped her voice another level or two. Jared could barely hear her. But considering that he genuinely believed she'd been abused he couldn't ignore anything that might give him clues to her past. He assumed Molly's father had been her abuser, but what if it had been someone from her hometown? He sat up, leaning toward the bathroom.

"I don't know a soul where we're going."

Jared frowned. He'd thought she was going home for Christmas. But apparently she was going to a town where she knew no one. That made no sense.

He waited in the dark, wondering if she'd run out of steam.

Suddenly she said, "But hey, I'm getting a house. And my grandmother's lawyer says it will be worth a bundle if I fix it up a bit before I sell it."

So that was it. She wasn't going to her hometown, but to her grandmother's hometown because she inherited her grandmother's house. That made sense—good sense—and also relieved Jared's mind a bit. She had an asset, something she could sell to secure her future. Even if she had been abused, she was moving on.

Her soft, almost childlike voice tiptoed into the quiet again. "Everything's going to be okay. There's no reason for me to be scared. Even if my dad had other kids, what can they do? Banish me from town? I'm not staying anyway. I'm going to fix up the house and hand it over to a Realtor."

Jared's mouth fell open in amazement. He wasn't a hundred percent sure how to sort through all that, except that the bottom line seemed to be that Elise was going to a town where she might have siblings. Siblings she didn't know.

He heard the sound of laughter, both Molly's and Elise's blending, and then Elise's voice changed, the way it did when she tickled Molly's tummy. "Now don't you go spinning fantasies about a family. We're each other's family. Just the two of us. That's enough. It's gotta be enough. Because expecting things that don't happen is how people get hurt."

Jared lay down on the bed again, his own heart hurting in his chest for her. She wasn't abused. She'd been deserted. Probably as a child if her father had been gone long enough for her to believe she could have siblings. And probably by the man who'd gotten her pregnant. Jared didn't know what had happened to her mother, but obviously she was out of the picture, too. Or Elise wouldn't have told Molly it was just the two of them.

It was no wonder Elise trusted no one.

"So how did you meet Michael?"

Elise glanced at Jared as he started the SUV and maneuvered out of the hotel parking lot. He'd been behaving strangely all morning. After sleeping until nine—which he swore he never did—he raced around the hotel room, dressing in what had to be record time for an adult male. She'd seen him shirtless, the dark whorls of the hair on his chest matching the dark hair on his head, reminding her of just how male he was. She'd heard the sounds of his electric razor. Sniffed the scent of his soap as it mingled with her shower gel—

And a hundred feminine longings that were better left alone tumbled through her. She was never so glad to get out of a hotel room in her life. Particularly since she'd noticed the way he'd looked at her the night before when he awoke to find her and Molly in the bathroom. He was every bit as attracted to her as she was to him.

Their attraction could make her suspicious of why he suddenly wanted to talk to her, but given his unusual personality it was entirely possible he'd have the opposite take on it than a normal guy. She'd bet her bottom dollar he believed that mindless conversation would keep both of them from thinking about an attraction neither one of them wanted.

Which actually made telling him a bit about herself a good idea.

"I was a waitress at Michael's favorite Italian restaurant."

"Ah. The little one on Juniper?"

She nodded.

"He goes there three times a week."

She laughed. "No kidding. And he came in at odd hours so there weren't any other customers and I had plenty of time to sit and talk. We got to know each other very well."

"Which is why he trusted you to watch his condo while he was gone?"

"Yes." Elise took a breath. If he could ask about her, maybe she could ask about him? "How did you meet Michael?"

"Waiting for the elevator."

"You became friends waiting for the elevator?"

Jared smiled. "No, we became friends when I didn't go to his Christmas party."

"*Didn't* go?"

"Every year he has a monumental Christmas party for everyone in the building. It's the biggest thing of the season. The first year I lived in the penthouse, he invited me, and even reminded me of the party several times when we met in front of the building elevators, but I didn't go."

This time Elise smiled. "And he wanted to know why."

"He was damned persistent about it, too."

She laughed. "I can only imagine."

"He came to the penthouse, demanding to know why I had blown him off, somehow got in the door, poured himself a drink and the next thing I knew we were talking about the Raiders."

"The Raiders?"

"Oakland Raiders. A football team. After that he dropped by with a six-pack one night to watch a basketball game and pretty soon it was all sports all the time for us. Two or three times a week, the nights I wasn't busy doing something for a client, he came over to watch whatever game was on, or I went to his apartment."

SUSAN MEIER 53

"And the next year you went to his party?"

He shook his head. "No."

Elise peered across the space at him. "No? He didn't win you over?"

"No, we became friends. Which was why he understood why I'd never come to his party."

"You don't like Christmas."

He glanced at her. "I'm just not much of a socializer."

She feigned shock. "You? I'm scandalized."

He smiled. The car was quiet for another few seconds, then Jared casually said, "So, you're going North Carolina?"

She nodded. "Mmm-hmm."

"So you must have family there?"

Molly began to fuss and Elise happily turned on her seat. This was the line, the thing she didn't care to discuss. So Molly had rescued her.

"She probably needs to be changed."

Jared said, "Next rest stop."

The SUV became quiet again, but Elise was glad. Molly had saved her from being rude to Jared, or admitting that she didn't want to talk about what she'd find in North Carolina. There was nothing to say anyway. She had no idea if she had family. No idea if the farm her grandmother left her was a palace or a pigsty. There was no sense talking about it when talking about it would only make her think about it. And she didn't want to think about it. But the silence didn't seem right, either.

After another few seconds, the quiet began to feel downright oppressive. Jared had been good to her and her baby for days. He wasn't nosy. He was only making conversation to keep both their minds off the taboo attraction. There were lots of things she could talk about without ever once mentioning any of her fears.

She took a breath. "I'm going to Four Corners because I inherited my grandmother's house."

"Hey, that's great!"

"You must have forgotten that my grandmother had to die for me to get her house."

He grimaced. "Sorry."

"It's okay. I didn't really know her."

"Oh."

He said it casually, but somehow the way that one little syllable came out of his mouth told her he already knew, and she shook her head. "You heard me talking last night."

"You were whispering, but I have really good ears." He waited a few beats then said, "I think it's kind of cool that your grandmother left you her house."

"God knows, I can certainly use the money I'll get when I sell it."

"Doesn't Molly's dad pay child support?"

She hadn't mentioned Patrick the night before so Jared was fishing. But they were in the realm of things he could guess or figure out on his own. So she'd answer; she simply wouldn't be too specific.

"Molly's dad is out of the picture."

"Your choice? His choice?"

"His. After I told him I was pregnant he left to go job hunting and never came home. I found him in Sacramento. Already living with another woman." She took a breath then deliberately smiled at Jared. "That was a long time ago. Losing him got lost in the shuffle of knowing I had to provide for a baby. Save some money. Get time off. That kind of stuff. For a while I scrambled, trying to set up everything for when I wouldn't be able to work, but waitresses don't make enough to save the amount I'd need to live on for weeks. That's when Michael came to the rescue."

"And then you inherited the house."

She nodded. "It couldn't have come at a better time." She took a breath. "The lawyer says the property is worth a nice sum and I figure I can sell it and get a jumpstart for me and Molly. So I'm going to Four Corners to make some repairs and put it on the market."

Jared swallowed hard. She spoke casually, trying to make him think the house was nothing but a transaction to her, but he knew the truth. For as much as she'd denied it to Molly the night before, she was hoping that she would find a family. Brothers and sisters. People who shared her bloodline.

"Where's your mom?"

"She died. The summer Patrick and I graduated from high school a cold she had wouldn't go away and before we knew it, she had pneumonia. She died in what seemed like the blink of an eye."

"I'm sorry."

She nodded. "It was awful. My mom was alone when she met my dad, so when he left, she and I were on our own. We never really had much of anything…so when she died—"

She stopped abruptly and Jared swallowed. He guessed she had been about to say she had been totally alone when her mother died, but she had stopped herself.

She took a breath. "So when she died, there was nothing. Just the old junk car she used for work that Pat and I drove to California." She laughed. "Where *it* died."

Jared felt that something inside him stir again. Right now a man who was whole and healthy, especially a lawyer accustomed to counseling people, would have the right words. But he had nothing. He knew just how wickedly life could treat some people. He knew why she didn't want to get her hopes up. It wouldn't be fair to pump her with possible wonderful outcomes only to watch her be disappointed.

Again.

"I'm sure everything will work out in Four Corners," he offered.

She snorted a laugh. "Right. The truth is the closer we get, the more sure I am that I'm just walking into another disappointment."

Not able to argue that, Jared didn't. He knew her fear because it was his own. He could pump himself with images of a happy reunion with his parents, parties with friends, giving and getting wonderful gifts. But he knew when he set foot on New York soil he'd be overwhelmed with sadness, images, people and places that would remind him of MacKenzie. Then he'd spend the weeks or even months after he returned to L.A. struggling with thoughts of how much he missed her and everything they'd lost.

The odds were better that Elise would find a family under her Christmas tree this year than that he'd find peace.

But he didn't think either one would happen. There was no sense pretending, only to have her hurt even worse when her dreams didn't come true.

They stopped once for Elise to change and feed Molly. Two hours later they ate lunch. The fast food restaurant they chose was nearly empty and oddly quiet. But it was after one o'clock on a workday. Life was going on as it should for the people of the State of Indiana. Jared watched Elise pick at her food, throwing away her French fries and eating only about half of her fish sandwich.

So at suppertime, he suggested they take a real break and eat somewhere nice, but Elise shook her head. "Nah. I can't afford to dillydally."

He knew the closer they got to their separation point in Pennsylvania, the more nervous she got, and suspected she wasn't eating because her stomach was tied in knots, so he didn't argue. They ate at another fast food restaurant and when she was done picking at her sandwich and fries, she stuffed the remains into the bag it came in, ready to throw it away.

"You know we're probably going to have to stop tonight and look for a bus station for you tomorrow." It pained him to be leaving her. Not just because he hated leaving her and her baby to a bus, but also because she was scared. Though their situations were totally different, he understood. He might be the only person on the planet who truly knew what she was going through.

"That's okay. But could we look for something a little cheaper this time?"

His eyes narrowed. "Are you running out of money?"

She laughed. "I told you Michael paid me very well and I saved most of the money, but I want to use it to make the repairs my grandmother's lawyer says the house will need if I want it to bring top dollar. So I have to be careful and not waste what I have."

I could give you some money. He almost said it. Mostly because he believed she'd struggled enough in one lifetime and deserved a break. But, though every fiber of his being longed to give her cash, he knew she wouldn't take it.

She rose from her seat and grabbed the handle of Molly's baby carrier. "I'll change her while you clear your stuff."

He looked up at her, catching the gaze of her pretty green eyes, wishing there was something he could do, some way he could help her that she couldn't refuse, argue, or return to him. And it suddenly dawned on him.

"How about if I meet you at the SUV?"

Elise said, "Great," then turned and walked to the bathroom.

Jared stuffed the remainder of his hamburger into his mouth, quickly cleared the table and all but ran to the SUV, where he got out the atlas. They had just crossed the Ohio border, having made good time after driving through and getting ahead of the one and only storm they'd encountered.

On the map of the United States, he traced the path east until he came to Cleveland because in Cleveland, Route 77 south went directly to North Carolina.

He glanced up just in time to see Elise approaching the car and tossed the atlas to the cargo space behind the backseat.

She settled Molly and climbed onto the passenger seat. Without a word, Jared got them back to the highway. The sky darkened as evening descended and Jared knew Elise was waiting for him to tell her to begin looking for a hotel.

Instead he kept driving. When they reached Cleveland, and he saw the sign for route 77 South he simply took the exit.

"Where are you going?"

"South." He peered over at her. "Unless you want to jump out and leave Molly with me, I'm taking you home for Christmas."

CHAPTER FOUR

APPREHENSION twisted Elise's stomach into a knot. All along she'd trusted him. But suddenly today he was chatty and now he'd changed their plans without consulting her. She was trapped in a car with a man who was basically a stranger, going somewhere different than what they'd planned.

Of course, he claimed he was taking her to North Carolina. But she'd seen the looks he'd given her the night before. She'd seen him studying her face as if suddenly realizing how attracted he was to her. She'd watched his gaze skim along the outline of her figure beneath her big T-shirt. And he knew she was alone. Someone no one would miss if she disappeared.

He didn't seem like the kind of guy to take advantage of a woman who was trapped in a car with him. But what did she know? Patrick was proof that she was a horrible judge of character.

She looked at the next road sign and mentally calculated how far they were from North Carolina. They were too far to drive there tonight. As Jared had already mentioned, they had one more hotel stop. Surely he didn't think she'd share a room with him again, just because they'd been forced to the night before?

She took a breath. She'd figure a way out of this. She had plenty of time.

But they went only another fifty miles before he shifted on the seat.

"I think it's time to stop."

"Great." Fine with her. As soon as he stopped, she could grab Molly and her things and bolt. If he thought she was so simple that she would share a room with him just because they had been forced to the night before, he was nuts. At the first opportunity, she was out of here.

He pulled the SUV in the parking lot of a family-owned motel and killed the engine. Elise calmly got out and began unbuckling Molly's baby carrier from the backseat. Jared walked over to where she stood at the car door rather than to the back of the SUV to retrieve her things as he normally did.

Fear made her breath shiver in her chest. "Aren't you going to get my diaper bag?"

"We'll get it after we check in."

"How about if I want it now?"

"Why?"

Her heart jumped to her throat. He wasn't giving her the chance to run. "This is a small motel. No matter what room the clerk assigns us, it will be walking distance."

"All right. Fine. Whatever."

He marched to the back of the SUV and snatched her things from the rear compartment. Blessed relief relaxed her muscles, until he headed for the door marked Office. She was still separated from her cooler and diaper bag with Molly's bottles and she couldn't run.

She scampered behind him, entering the small, dingy office on his heels. He wouldn't beat her so easily. Once she was close enough to her things that she could grab them, she would. Then she was out of here. She wasn't sure where she'd go, but she certainly wasn't staying with a guy she totally mistrusted.

Jared walked up to the counter, carrying her things in his left hand. The middle-aged clerk turned away from the TV. Her voice was bored and tired when she said, "Can I help you?"

"Yes. We'd like rooms for the night."

She glanced at Elise and the baby, then back at Jared. "Rooms?"

"Yes, my friend and I both need a room."

Elise stepped closer to the counter. He hadn't tried to get her to share a room?

The clerk turned and tapped on a keyboard. "I'll need a credit card."

Elise took another step toward the counter. "I'd like to pay with cash."

Before the clerk could open her mouth, Jared said, "Take her cash and use my credit card to guarantee any other expenses she might make."

"I'm not going to make any other expenses. I'm guessing the place doesn't have room service and I'm not going to use the phone—"

"The clerk doesn't know that," Jared said, handing his credit card over to the woman with a smile. "And if you're not planning to use the phone or do any damage to the room, then her using my number is just a formality."

The clerk looked past Jared at Elise with a smile. "It's true."

Jared turned to her and softly, reassuringly said, "I'm just saving us all a little hassle."

Feeling like an idiot, Elise swallowed. "Okay."

"Okay."

They got their room keys and Jared hoisted the straps of her bags onto his shoulder. On the way to her room, he said, "You don't trust me at all, do you?"

"I don't trust anybody." She tried to say it lightly but even she heard the defensive note in her own voice. The guy had been nothing but nice to her, but she couldn't stop her suspicions. Everybody she'd trusted in her life had let her down. Suspicion was her natural reaction to everything. She could accept a ride across the country because Jared was going that way, too. It wasn't really a sacrifice for him, just a bit of an inconvenience because of Molly. But he got nothing from taking her all the way home.

Jared shook his head. "Tonight, I'm too tired to care."

She unlocked her hotel room door and walked inside. There were two standard-issue double beds in the small, but reasonably clean room. Jared tossed her bags to the first bed and turned to the door. "Good night, Elise."

Without another word, he closed the door behind him. Elise put Molly's baby carrier on the bed and removed her coat then undressed Molly. She felt foolish for being suspicious of him, but what choice did she have? Trust him? Count on him? Then be let down again?

She didn't think so.

* * *

The next morning, they grabbed a cup of coffee in the hotel lobby and were on the road before seven. Jared didn't speak, except to tell her that when she was hungry she could look for a restaurant. She said, "Okay," and the SUV became quiet again. Just as it had been the first few days. But this morning was different. She'd insulted him by mistrusting him and his motives for taking her the whole way to North Carolina. She'd continued to be a thorn in his side when he'd had to explain the whole credit card issue to her the night before. Now he was tired of her. Tired of explaining himself to her. Tired, she supposed, of proving himself to her. And insulted that she'd obviously believed he wanted to sleep with her. That he would take advantage of her.

Around ten o'clock, Elise's stomach growled and she pointed out a sign for a restaurant just off the interstate. Without comment, Jared took the exit and in ten minutes they were sitting in a comfortable booth. While Elise and Jared ate, Molly chewed her teething ring. They didn't speak. Their booth was so silent that Elise wasn't surprised that Jared pulled out a cell phone, after they'd finished their pancakes and were waiting for the waitress to bring their bill.

Telling herself she wasn't trying to make conversation because she was embarrassed about being suspicious of him, but was genuinely curious, Elise said, "Your cell phone hasn't rang in four days?"

He glanced over at her. His gray eyes cautious. "I had it turned off."

"Can you do that?"

He put his gaze back on the phone. "There's an off switch."

Elise sighed. "I know *that*. I'm just saying that your parents might have been trying to call."

"My parents would know I couldn't take their calls because I was driving. More likely if anybody called it would have been clients."

"Oh, that's right. Those high-powered types you do the big deals for."

"Right."

"So what's it like?"

He peered up at her again. "What's what like?"

She sighed. "Come on. I feel bad about mistrusting you. Throw me a bone. Make meaningless conversation so I won't feel guilty for the rest of the trip."

"How can you mistrust somebody who's doing you a favor?"

She could have told him that she'd seen the looks he'd given her and knew exactly how attracted he was to her. She could have said that she'd been afraid he'd ask her to do something about the need that pulsed between them. She could have also admitted that her brain had jumped to that place because she'd been feeling the attraction, too. Especially when he ran around their hotel room, shirtless, trying to get dressed. She could be honest and admit that something about him easily awoke her sleeping femininity and that scared her. So she'd panicked.

Instead she took the less complicated way out. "It's very easy for me to mistrust you—to mistrust period. A little over a year ago the father of my child told me he was going upstate to look for a job and he never came back. So shoot me if I'm a little suspicious." She took a quick breath, not wanting him to have time to comment on that, and repeated her question, nudging him to forgive her simply by getting them back to normal conversation, rather than making a big deal out of it. "So what's it like representing movie stars?"

He studied her face for a few seconds, obviously debating, then pulled in a breath, and said, "It's a lot like babysitting."

Because that hadn't been what she'd expected him to say, she burst out laughing. "Babysitting?"

"Yeah, babysitting. When rich people get into trouble, they don't call a friend or their shrink, they call their lawyer. That's me."

"So you don't spend your days reading contracts and negotiating with movie studios?"

"I do some of that. But agents handle most of it. Lots of my work is hands-on."

"Hands-on?"

"You know how some of Hollywood's young super-stars keep doing things like getting pulled over for DUIs and going in and out of rehab?"

She nodded.

"That's my job."

"You arrange the rehab?"

"No. I fix things behind the scenes. Though I represent them at their hearings and trials, I also do things like take decent clothes to them so they don't come out of jail looking like they're coming off a bender or dressed like a fifty-cent hooker."

"Fifty-cent?" She laughed again. "Isn't that a little harsh?"

He rolled his eyes. "Lately most of my clients' tastes

run toward bordello not boardroom. Not even ballroom. Not even bar. Bordello."

"That is so cool."

He sniffed a laugh. "Cool to have clients who don't even have the common sense to behave when the whole world is watching, hoping for them to do something stupid?"

"No. That part's kinda weird. But don't you think it's cool to know what to do to get somebody out of trouble?"

"Yeah. Not all my clients are that extreme. Lots of them are good people." He caught her gaze again. "I don't mind picking up the pieces for them. They're busy. They're always in the spotlight. And a lot of times through no fault of their own, they can find themselves in the wrong place at the wrong time and they need somebody to fix things."

"Fix things?"

"I spend a lot of my time sneaking people out of places."

"What kind of places?"

"Places like a director's office when a client is negotiating for a movie without their agent because they're on the verge of firing one and hiring another. Out of the wrong house at the wrong hour of the night when a client sees a photographer outside. Out of doctor's offices when the press is waiting for them on the sidewalk."

"Don't they have bodyguards for this kind of stuff?"

He laughed, and settled comfortably on the booth seat. "This all goes back to calling the lawyer instead of your friend. Everybody's so lawsuit-happy these days that my clients sometimes check with me before they sneeze."

She shook her head. This was why he kept being nice to her. "You're a rescuer."

"More of a babysitter."

She shook her head again. "No. You're a rescuer. That's why you're taking me home."

"Could we just say I like to do good deeds?"

"No. You don't *like* to do good deeds. Otherwise, we'd see you around the apartment complex more. You only do the good deeds you feel compelled to do." She took a breath. "You got to know me and Molly on the trip and you couldn't leave us. You had to take us home."

He glanced down at his place mat then back up at her again, his gray eyes dark and serious. "Is that so bad?"

"It's not bad for me. It's a lucky break for me."

The waitress walked over with the bill. Her Southern accent wove through her words as she said, "Thanks, ya'all have a good morning, now."

Jared said, "Thanks," and reached in his pants pocket for his wallet.

Elise got her wallet out of her purse. Because they'd ordered the same breakfast, she divided the cost in half and tossed enough money to pay her share plus a tip on the little tray holding the bill.

"You being a rescuer is a lucky break for me," she said, bringing their conversation back because she was curious. "But I've got to wonder how good it is for you."

"Taking you home adds another day or two to my trip. Cuts another day or two off the time I have to spend in New York."

"No. I'm talking about your job. Why do you rescue people professionally?"

He tossed enough bills to cover his share of the cost of breakfast to the little black tray. "Money."

"Right."

"I'm serious. I make a lot of money doing what I do."

"And you like the money?"

He nodded. "Hell, yeah. Plus, it keeps me busy."

She studied his face. His pretty gray eyes that seemed to see everything. The sharp angles of his cheekbones that added an edge of masculinity to a face that otherwise might have been too pretty. He was so damned handsome it amazed her that one of his equally attractive movie-star clients hadn't snapped him up.

Unless he didn't want to be snapped up?

He kept delaying his trip to New York. He'd said he wasn't much on socializing. He *liked* working with clients who called him at all hours of the day and night. He wanted to be busy. The same way she had been when she was pregnant and didn't want to sit at home reminded that Pat wasn't coming back, and trying to forget that she'd been kidding herself for the six years they lived together—avoiding the truth that Patrick was worthless. And she should have seen it years before.

"So what are you running from?"

"Excuse me?"

"I'm going to Four Corners, facing God knows what kind of reception from the people of the small town where my dad grew up because I'm tired of sitting around thinking about the fact that I trusted the wrong guy. You moved to California from New York City. Three thousand miles. Whatever you want to forget it's got to be big."

He slid across the bench seat of the booth, but

before he could stand, Elise caught his wrist. "I've been telling you bits and pieces of my life for the past few days. You can give me a few pieces of yours."

"I told you about my clients."

"But you're not going to tell me why you're running?"

"I'm not running. I settled in California because I'm paid well there."

"Don't even bother trying to tell me you're the only lawyer in New York City who *wasn't* paid well."

"I was a prosecutor. A civil employee. I did okay. But I didn't make millions. Now I make millions. Enough said."

She knew it was more than that, but she didn't argue. His entire demeanor changed when he put up his guard. The light in his eyes went out. His mouth firmed. His shoulders went back, as if he were preparing for battle. She could see there was no point in pushing when she'd get no answers.

They got back into the SUV and before she could occupy her mind with anything else, her own troubles pressed in on her. The closer they got to Four Corners the more nervous she got.

"This is why I decided to drive you," Jared said when they were about halfway through the state of North Carolina. They'd passed the exit for the road that would take them to Raleigh, her bus's destination, and now *he* was getting nervous, concerned she'd become so afraid that she let her destination go by.

"You're quiet. You're sullen. I'm guessing you're changing your mind about fixing your grandmother's house for sale. Maybe even considering selling it as is, just to avoid what you might find when you get to Four Corners."

"What are you? Psychic?"

"Nope. Just so familiar with extreme emotions that I know how to read people." He pointed at the big green exit sign at the side of the road. "We've already passed the exit for Raleigh. I recognize the bus might not have gone directly to your grandma's small town, but I'm starting to worry we passed your exit and you simply didn't tell me."

"It's the next one."

Her voice was so quiet that he stopped pushing. He knew the signs of a person on the edge and if he kept nudging she really could change her mind, or sell her grandmother's house on the blind, as is, when simple repairs might get her a lot more money. If he pushed and she bolted, he'd be the one to blame.

"Did it ever occur to you that your grandmother leaving you the house is a huge statement?"

"Yes."

He glanced over, saying nothing but letting her know with his expression that he expected more of an answer than that.

She sighed. "I think she's telling me that my dad had no other kids. That there was no one else to leave it to."

"You don't think she's saying that she's sorry for never contacting you? Or that maybe she's trying to make up for the fact that her own son never supported you?"

She shrugged. "I think it's more probable that he had no other children and my grandmother didn't want the family property to revert to the government. I think they're saying I'm better than nothing."

Her words were soft, and hit Jared like an arrow to his heart. His exile had been his choice. Anytime in the past five years, he could have gone home. He *wanted* to be alone. Elise didn't. And there was nothing he could do to help her.

His attention on the exit, he said nothing. At the Stop sign at the bottom he looked over at her. "Left?"

She nodded and pointed at the green road sign with an arrow left, announcing that the town was twenty miles away. "Sign says it's left."

He pulled onto the road. "So you don't think your grandmother wanted to give you the house so you'd have a jumpstart on life?"

"Whether she wanted to give me a jumpstart or not, that's exactly what she's doing." She took a breath. "But it really doesn't matter why she gave me the house. The end result is good and that's what counts."

Jared peered over. "Yet you're still nervous."

"There's always the possibility that my dad had more kids and that my grandmother had her reasons for not giving them the property. Maybe she was rich and had other things to leave to them? Or maybe she hated them and decided to spite them by giving me the farm when they wanted it?" She sighed heavily. "Which would mean I could be walking into a nasty situation that includes a court battle."

Glad that she'd finally admitted it so they could talk about it, he glanced at her and saw her as she really was. Vulnerable. Scared. Alone.

"I know a good lawyer."

This time the laugh that bubbled from her was genuine. "You're going to New York and then back to California."

"I'll find someone for you."

"You'll be long gone before this all plays out."

And that troubled him. Because she was right. She could have half brothers and sisters who could very well sue for part of their grandmother's estate and they might not surface until she had the house fixed, willing to get part of the money, but not to do any of the work. He had to figure out a way to get to the bottom of her family situation before he left her.

CHAPTER FIVE

THEY were quiet again until they entered Four Corners. Jared looked around in awe. It wasn't that he'd never been in a rural town before, but this one could have been a Christmas card. Victorian houses with white fences were decorated with red ribbons and evergreen wreaths. The streetlights and parking meters were spiraled in tinsel that glistened in the late afternoon sun. Yards displayed nativity scenes and fat Santas with sleighs.

Elise pulled a letter from her purse. "We need to go to the lawyer's office to pick up the key."

"You have directions or an address on that letter?"

"Main Street."

He laughed. "Of course. It's a small town. Everything important is on Main Street."

When they located the lawyer's office Jared wasn't surprised to see it was the first floor of a white Victorian house, decorated for Christmas with generous evergreen wreaths with plump red bows in the windows and silver bells hanging around the door.

As they walked up the wood plank porch steps, Elise said, "I keep waiting for someone to drive down the street in a horse-drawn carriage."

Jared laughed. "I hear ya. But it's cute, you know?" He glanced down the street. "Homey."

He opened the door for Elise and they walked into a foyer that had been turned into a reception room with the addition of a matching antique desk and cabinet and a thick Persian rug.

Behind the desk a woman around fifty stared at a computer monitor as her fingers clicked away on the keyboard. Without looking at them she said, "May I help you?"

"I'm Elise McDermott."

The older woman turned from the computer. Her face brightened. "Debbie McDermott's granddaughter?"

"Yes."

She picked up the phone and hit two buttons. "Mr. Collins, Debbie's granddaughter is here." She paused. "Will do."

Returning the receiver to the cradle, she smiled at Elise. "You can go on in." She motioned to the baby. "I'll be happy to keep her while you talk with Mr. Collins."

Elise shied away, reminding Jared of the woman he'd offered a ride across the country to. Every time they entered a new situation, she reverted back to the little girl who'd been left by her dad, teenager who lost her mom and pregnant young woman who hadn't been wanted by the father of her child.

Holding Molly protectively, Elise smiled and said, "Thanks, but no. We're fine."

As they walked into the office, the aging lawyer rose from behind a shiny mahogany desk. With his white hair and moustache, red cheeks and round tummy that stretched his black vest to the limits, he reminded Jared of Santa Claus. When Jared saw the jar of red and green jelly beans on his desk, he smiled.

"Good afternoon, Elise. I'm George Collins. Sit. Sit!" He motioned to the two captain's chairs in front of his desk.

Elise didn't sit. "We've been driving for days. So if you could give us the key so we can settle Molly, I'd appreciate it."

George kindly said, "Of course," as he reached for the handle of a drawer on his left. "You have the ID I asked you to bring, don't you? Proof that you're Elise McDermott."

As she had on their trip, she handed Molly to Jared before she rifled through her purse and produced a birth certificate and driver's license. The license had both the California address where Collins had located her and her photo on it.

George looked down at the license, up at her, then back down at the license before he said, "Good enough." He handed the key across the desk, along with a piece of paper. "The gold key opens the house. The others are for outbuildings. The paper has directions to the farm. Stop in tomorrow and we'll get all the official estate documents signed."

Key and directions in hand, Elise turned to go, but Jared couldn't leave yet. He wasn't her lawyer, so he couldn't come back later and ask questions on his own. The only way to satisfy his curiosity would be with Elise in the room.

"Mr. Collins, Elise didn't really know her family. Can you answer a few questions?" He didn't pause for a yes or no in case Elise protested before he got everything out. "Is her dad around? Does she have brothers and sisters?"

Elise froze. She knew Jared's intentions were good, but this was none of his business. She wasn't ready. And especially not like this. Her entire life had been a series of surprise revelations. *Your dad's not coming home. Your mom is dead. I don't want to be a daddy. You're on your own.*

She didn't want or need another one.

Mr. Collins smiled sympathetically at Elise. "Do you have time to hear this?"

Elise resisted the urge to gape at him. *Time?* This wasn't about time. It was about fear. But now that the questions were out on the table, she would look like a ninny for dodging them. Besides, from the sympathetic expression on his face, she already knew the answers were bad.

She tried to smile. "Yes. I have time."

He drew a breath. "Your father is dead and you have no siblings."

Elise's knees weakened and she was glad Jared was holding Molly. She lowered herself to one of the two captain's chairs in front of the desk.

"I'm sorry, Elise, but the farm reverted to you by default. Because you had been estranged I didn't think it necessary to explain that there was no will. Everybody knew Miz McDermott's only child—your dad— had died years ago. When we hired a private investigator the way we normally do, we expected him to come up empty and for the farm to be sold for taxes. But low and behold, there you were. Your parents' marriage license and your birth certificate were easy to find public records." He laughed lightly. "*You* weren't so easy to find, but the birth certificate told us you existed so we looked for your driver's license records and when we got to the State of California, there you were."

"My grandmother didn't have a will?" she whispered, hardly believing she could speak, as so many realizations hit her. She really was alone. Her grandmother hadn't cared about her. No one cared about her.

"No. When I mentioned preparing one for her, she always said next time. But I'd spoken to her often enough and about personal things that she would have talked about you to me if she had known you existed."

"Which explains why she never called me to tell me my father was dead."

Mr. Collins's sympathetic smile faded and his eyes softened with compassion as he met her gaze. "She would have wanted to know you, Elise. I'm sorry that she didn't. And I'm sorry to have to break all this to you."

Elise rose and pasted on a smile, picking herself up and metaphorically dusting herself off, the way she always did. "Hey, that's okay. This was one of the scenarios I'd run through my mind." She batted a hand in dismissal. "I'm fine."

The old man nodded. "Good."

"I'll see you tomorrow to sign those papers."

"It doesn't have to be tomorrow or even the day after. Should be someday soon, though."

Elise walked out of the office and it wasn't until they were at the door of the house that she realized she didn't have Molly. Jared did. She turned and simply took her child, her only living relative, from his arms and hugged her as they stepped out into the North Carolina afternoon.

They silently walked down the street where tinsel on the parking meters glistened in the overly bright sun and every storefront was decorated for the holiday.

When she opened the SUV door to put Molly inside, Jared was suddenly at her side. "You don't need to hover. I'm not going to faint."

He stepped back a few feet, but stayed behind her. "I know. But you got some surprising news in there."

With Molly settled, she pulled out of the SUV, slammed the back door and opened the front door to climb inside. Before she did, she turned to Jared and said, "Surprising to you maybe. But my whole life has been like this. I don't even have siblings to get into a good fight with over the family estate."

She'd thought the irony would make her laugh. Instead an unexpected avalanche of anger over-whelmed her. Why was life always so cruel to her? And why couldn't Jared have waited to ask? Why couldn't he give her a few days to get adjusted to the fact that her grandmother didn't know she existed before she had to learn that she had no one? What the hell was he doing in her business anyway!

"Why did you do that!"

"Do what? Ask about your family?"

"Yes." She all but spat the word. "You couldn't

give me at least until Christmas to discover that I was alone? You couldn't give me one Christmas to pretend I had a family?"

She stood by the door of the SUV, which sat between two parking meters gilded in glittering tinsel. Everything around them seemed to be eagerly awaiting snow. But she was as angry and unforgiving as a hot August sun.

Jared combed his fingers through his hair. "Look, I have experience with things like this. Coming right out and asking was the best way to handle it."

She gaped at him. "Really? It was best for me to spend my first Christmas with Molly having to explain that someday *she'll* be as alone as I am?"

"No. But—"

"No buts! Dear God, Jared! It's just about Christmas. You couldn't give me a week of feeling somebody out there might want me?"

"I couldn't leave you without knowing whether or not you needed a lawyer."

She laughed bitterly. "So what you really cared about was easing your own conscience so you could drop me without feeling guilty." She shook her head. "For such a braggart rescuer, you screwed this one up big time."

Jared opened his mouth to say something, but snapped it closed. He had a horrible feeling she was right. No. He *knew* she was right. He knew she wanted a home, family. Yet he thought of his concerns first. If she needed a lawyer, he wanted to be here and he didn't trust her to allow him to lag behind for the time it would take for her to gather her courage and ask

Collins about her family. He had to know today. So he'd asked.

Selfish. Which absolutely amazed him. He couldn't remember the last time he put his needs above a client's. Yet that's what he'd done. He'd thought of himself first. He'd done it because he was desperate to help her, but he hadn't looked at her situation objectively and he'd made a mistake.

He rounded the hood of the SUV, yanked open his door and slid onto the seat, behind the steering wheel. This was the second time with Elise that his emotions had more than edged into the picture. The first time was in the hotel room when sexual urges he hadn't felt in years nearly overwhelmed him. But at least he'd controlled those. Would that he'd been smart enough to control the impulse to put his nose into her business at the lawyer's office.

"Can I have the directions?"

Elise waved the paper at him. "No need. Just follow this road out of town and after two miles look for a mailbox that's shaped like a cat."

Jared turned the key and started the SUV engine. "Good enough." He turned to the right and continued to drive down Main Street. The little town was so beautiful, so quaint, so perfectly decorated for the holiday that he felt like an even bigger fool for not taking the date into consideration when he asked if she had family. Some rescuer he was.

"So your grandmother's mailbox is a cat?" He laughed, trying desperately to lighten the mood so that eventually he could ask for forgiveness. "She must have been a real cat person."

But Elise didn't reply. She didn't laugh. She didn't tell him to let her alone. She simply sat there, staring straight ahead, not moving, until she unexpectedly faced him. "We need milk."

He damned near breathed a sigh of relief, except telling him she needed milk only meant she wasn't so angry she'd forget about her baby.

Seeing a small grocery store a few buildings down the street, he pointed at it and said, "We'll stop there and I'll just run in and get some." When he pulled into a parking space, he shoved the gearshift into Park but left the keys in the ignition. At this point, if she wanted to take his car, he'd let her.

But when he jumped out Elise also climbed out.

"I thought I was getting this?"

She shook her head. "I'm fine."

He groaned. "Stop saying you're fine. I know you're not fine. This time it's my fault—"

But Elise didn't even look at him. She simply got Molly out of the car seat and marched into the store to the coolers in the back. Jared scrambled after her. She grabbed a gallon of milk, turned and walked to the checkout counter.

"Good afternoon!" The tall, bald, fifty-something clerk boomed his greeting as Elise set her milk on the counter.

She didn't reply. Jared could see she was all but oblivious to her surroundings, so he said, "Good afternoon."

"You're new around here." He grabbed the milk and tapped the price into an old-fashioned cash register. "I'm Pete. I own this store. If there's anything you need. You can probably find it here. If not, there's a general store—sort of like an old five-and-dime—eight stores down to the right." He winked at Elise. "And if you can't find it there, you come back and ask me and I'll put out feelers and find it for you."

Elise handed her money to him without saying a word. Jared's worry meter, which had already hit the height of what it could register, began shimmying, as if about to explode. Not because he thought she'd have a fit of temper, but because he recognized the signs of a person shutting down. Going into her shell. Retreating from the world. And she couldn't do that. She had a baby to care for.

Elise grabbed the milk and headed for the door. Jared smiled at Pete. "Thanks."

Frowning at silent Elise, Pete said, "You're welcome."

But Elise was already walking out of the store. She was spiraling into a black pit of depression, the one he'd lived in for years, and it was his fault. If he'd let her find out about her family on her own, she probably would have been able to handle it. Instead he'd pushed.

He ran to the SUV, jumped in and started the engine, his mind racing faster than any turbine could. He had to fix this. But how? How did a person unring a bell? Take back a question? Take back answers she already knew?

He turned them in the direction of the farm again and in what seemed like seconds they were out of town, on a stretch of highway that fronted farmland. Two miles of country road took them past three small farms and finally Elise pointed at a mailbox shaped like a cat, beside a tree-lined lane.

He maneuvered the car onto the gravel road, liking the

healthy trees and privacy Elise's property had, but when they reached the end of the driveway and got to the house, the idyllic landscape changed to weeds and bramble.

Bushes and shrubs had overgrown their boundaries and were edging into the tall weeds in what Jared guessed should have been a yard. Two rusting cars sat by a wooden garage that was missing boards and needed painting.

Jared's mouth fell open in horror. "I can see why Mr. Collins suggested you fix this up before you put it on the market. Looks like you've got your work cut out for you."

Elise said nothing, just opened her car door and jumped out, turning to get Molly. Cursing in his head, Jared followed suit, going to the back of the SUV to get her things.

The house itself didn't look bad until they got close. Then he saw that the exterior siding had faded and, like the outbuildings, needed a coat of paint. Two of the boards of the wooden steps leading to the plank porch were broken.

He was about to leave her alone and sad, in a place that wouldn't jog her internal optimism. If anything, staying at this farm could make her situation seem all the more hopeless.

When Elise silently unlocked the front door, the pretty beige ceramic tile and cherrywood stairway in the foyer cheered him. The worst thing he saw as they passed the living room and formal dining room was the coating of dust on the obviously old furniture.

In the kitchen, she glanced around, taking in the table and chairs, toaster, microwave and coffeemaker that sat around the room. "Looks like I inherited the furniture, too."

Though he was glad she had spoken, his panicked mind reminded him this was it. She was at her destination, and he wasn't staying. He was supposed to drop her and go.

Glancing around, grasping for any straw of a reason to stay, he pointed at a water mark on the ceiling. "Yeah, you might have inherited a furnished house, but that stain says something's leaking."

"Maybe the bathroom is above the kitchen and the bath overflowed or the toilet leaked?" She opened a cupboard door. "Oh, look. Whoever cleaned out the house left the dishes."

"You call this clean?"

She shrugged. "There's nothing thrown around. There are no dirty dishes. No day-to-day clutter. It's just dusty. So, yeah. I think somebody cleaned." After opening a few more cupboard doors, she faced Jared with a slight smile. "There's no food but I have a furnished house."

She said it with such a lilt of awe in her voice that Jared got his first indication that she might be okay. Still, he knew what a good actress she was. She could have already guessed that he wouldn't leave her in this condition. She might be pretending to be recovering from the news so he would go. Leave her alone. And risk that she'd become as he had become. A recluse. Someone who pretended her way through life and never really lived.

He licked his suddenly dry lips. Now was not the time to dissect his past. Elise's present was more important. If the best he could do was get a repairman or contractor out to this farm with her to force her into the activity of fixing her house so she wouldn't sink any further into despair, then that's what he'd do.

"You have a furnished house with a leaky bathroom." He turned back toward the hall. "Let's go check this out."

Walking up the steps, he didn't see any cracks in the plaster on the walls. The steps didn't creak. The floor beneath the carpeting in the hall appeared to be solid. But a stain on the ceiling in the upstairs bathroom indicated the roof had leaked.

Finally a problem he could sink his rescuer teeth into. If he exaggerated this just a fraction, he might be able to talk her into letting him take her to the bed-and-breakfast they'd passed in town. That would be even better than getting a contractor out here. At a bed-and-breakfast, she'd have company, a bubbly proprietor whose job it was to make sure guests were comfortable and happy. She wouldn't be alone or have time to brood.

"You aren't planning to stay in the house while you fix it up, are you?"

"Actually I am."

He pointed to the ceiling. "That says you can't."

She laughed. "You forget I've been poor most of my life. I know that one stain doesn't mean I have to leave."

Standing by a white sink accented by shiny black wall tile and the black and white mosaic floor of the eight-by-eight room, he faced her. "All right, Elise. This is no time to be stubborn. *You* have a baby and this plumbing and roof leak. You might be able to tough it out, but do you want Molly staying here?"

"I think the plumbing might just be a result of nobody living here for the past six months."

"And the roof?"

"I'll get it fixed." She glanced around. "Obviously I have to fix a lot of things to bring the value of the property up for when I sell it. I'll just do the roof and plumbing first."

"I'm not letting you stay here if this roof could fall in on you." He strode out of the bathroom, into the upstairs hallway, looking for a pull-down ladder to the attic. Not finding one, he marched into the first bedroom. The sheets and pillows had been removed from a double bed, revealing a plastic covered mattress. Somebody had obviously cleared out the personal items after Elise's grandmother's death. What was left was a shell. Sort of like Elise's life. She had everything but people. Everything but personal contact. And he was making sure she had some before he left. Even if he had to exaggerate.

A dusty dresser and mirror vanity, each sat by a closed door in the bedroom. Opening the first door, he found a closet stacked with linens. Opening the second, he found the stairs to the attic.

Because he hoped to exaggerate the roof's condition into an excuse for her to leave, he couldn't let her come up with him. So he pointed at the baby she held and said, "You stay here," then climbed the steps.

Layer upon layer of dry dust on old furniture confirmed that the problem with the roof was confined to one area. Luckily nothing had been stored in that spot.

He glanced around, surveying the underside of the roof again, feeling very much like the carpenter he'd been while working his way through college and law school. The roof wasn't really bad, but it was old and needed to be replaced. The house was small, two story, which meant it wasn't a big job. A crew could replace it in a few days. With a little help *he* could replace it in a few days.

He peered around again. He *could* replace this roof in a few days. And if he stayed, she wouldn't be alone. He smiled. Maybe he shouldn't exaggerate the problem, but downplay it? It was so close to Christmas that even if she tried to get a contractor, most were probably already busy. If he got her to call and nobody had time in their schedule to do the work, he could wheedle his way into staying.

He walked down the stairs. Elise stood in the bedroom, waiting for him.

"Okay. I think I might have jumped the gun on whether or not you can live here. I have to check out the basement foundation before I officially pronounce it livable, but if you get the roof fixed as soon as possible, I think you can stay."

"Great. Give me your cell phone. I'll call a roofer while you go to the basement."

"The basement can wait. I want to stay with you while you call a roofer."

She sighed in exasperation. "You don't have to make sure I'm calling! I'm fixing the house up for sale. I'll be replacing the roof eventually anyway. I have no reason to lie about calling someone."

"I know. I just want to stay in case you need help."

She turned on a huff of exasperated air, carried Molly to the kitchen and rummaged in a drawer for a phone book. Jared handed her his cell phone to make the call and took Molly.

But as he expected, no one was available. Elise worked her way down the entire line of contractors in the slim phone book and not one even had time to do an estimate.

"Here." He handed Molly back to her and took the phone. "Let me try."

"Do you think that I'm lying when I tell you everybody's booked?"

"No. You have no reason to lie." But, he had ulterior motives for checking on a roofer himself. If she watched him honestly try to get someone here and still fail, she wouldn't argue when he told her he could do the roof himself.

"But I do think that with a little persuasion I could have somebody here tomorrow." Like a poker player trying to sucker his opponent into betting when he knew he had the winning hand, he sweetened the pot. "Then you'd be rid of me."

"What kind of persuasion?"

"I'm a fix-it guy, remember? A rescuer. If I can't sweet-talk one silly roofer, I don't deserve my big salary."

He dialed the first number in the phone book's line of roofing contractors and the receptionist told him that her boss and his crew were busy and not in the office. Jared suggested it might be worth her boss's while to return his call, and she laughed, saying that they had so much business that the offer of extra money wasn't an incentive for her employer anymore.

So he moved to the next contractor. Because it was a bigger company he was transferred from the receptionist to a project manager who, in spite of the extra money Jared offered, told him all his teams were booked. Just as Elise had, Jared worked through the line of contractors without any luck.

Elise smirked at him. "Well, it looks like money doesn't talk as loudly here as it does in L.A."

"I can normally get anybody to do anything."

"Welcome to the real world."

"Actually this sort of is my real world. I told you I got through law school working in construction." He took a breath. "So, I have a proposition for you."

Her eyes narrowed.

"I'll fix the roof."

She laughed. "You!"

"Hey, I'm serious. I worked my way through law school in construction. A roof is very simple. And the fresh air will be good for me."

She only gaped at him.

"Give me five days." He headed for the stairs again. If he was going to do this he needed to measure a few things. "If I can find a crew, I'll be out of your hair in no time. This doesn't have to be a big deal."

"Jared, you have only till Christmas. Your parents—"

In the middle of the downstairs hall, he stopped and faced her. "My parents will be proud of me for helping you."

"I'm not going to be responsible for delaying your trip again."

"You're not. It's my choice. You need a new roof. I know how to put on a new roof. Let me go into town and see if I can hire a few guys to help, and I can easily be home before Christmas."

She sighed then met Jared's gaze. "Fine."

Her easy acquiescence caused his lips to lift into a smile. "You're letting me do it?"

"Do I have a choice?"

He turned and started up the stairs. "Not really. But I was at least expecting an argument."

She sighed. "I'm being realistic. I might be able to go a day or two without a new roof, but I can't keep a baby here for the weeks it would take until one of the contractors is free."

Starting up the steps, he laughed. "I like you when you're pragmatic." He really did. Not just because her common sense separated her from the ditzy people he normally dealt with but because her simple way of looking at life made it easy for him to forgive himself. For once he didn't feel the need to do penance.

That would have stopped him, except he was beginning to realize that around Elise he was a totally different guy. His normal self. Not the plastic man who took care of Hollywood's elite. Not the man surrounded by walls that insulated him from real life. Just himself.

Being himself would mean trouble when he got to New York. But he wasn't in New York. He was in Four Corners, North Carolina. He could be himself. He'd figure out why it was so easy to be himself later, when he actually had some time to think about it.

"But before you do anything, you have to agree that I'm paying for the materials."

"No problem. Give me the rest of the day to look for a crew and check out the hardware store. Hopefully Four Corners has a home improvement center or lumberyard close by, too. I'll buy what I need and happily bring you the sales slip."

She jostled Molly on her hip nervously. "I feel as if I'm aiding and abetting a fugitive."

He stopped and looked down at her, holding up his hand as if swearing to a promise. "Nothing like that."

"One of these days you're going to have to tell me about your past."

"I told you my past. I was an assistant district attorney. I left New York because I wanted the sunshine of L.A. and the money."

She said, "Yeah, right."

But he was already the rest of the way up the steps. From the top, he called down to her, "See if you can't find a pencil and a tape measure. I can't buy supplies until I figure out how much I'll need."

CHAPTER SIX

JARED drove through Four Corners convinced the little town was a world of its own. Filled with well-maintained houses and smiling residents, it exuded an old-fashioned charm that seemed to seep into his soul and make him feel at home in a place he'd never been before. But that didn't mean the people who lived in these pretty houses weren't endowed with normal curiosity. As soon as they realized someone had inherited the McDermott place, everyone from church ladies welcoming her to town to people hoping to sweet-talk her into selling the farm could come by the house.

Still, anyone visiting was a good idea. A slow stream of neighbors with casseroles would keep Elise from having too much time to dwell on her lack of family. So he had to get the ball rolling on that and the first step was letting people know she had arrived without making a big deal of it.

He parked on the street, fed a meter spiraled in gold tinsel and walked up to the diner. He opened the door and sleigh bells jingled announcing his arrival.

"Good afternoon, mister," a waitress wiping down the front counter greeted him.

"Good afternoon." He glanced around at the tinsel

on the counter and the evergreen decorated with multicolored balls and twinkling lights that stood in the corner. The little restaurant reminded him of a New York City diner he had frequented in his other life. He had a fleeting thought that MacKenzie would have loved this place, but just as quickly remembered he was here for Elise. She and Molly needed a roof—and some company.

He sat at the counter.

"What'll it be?"

"Coffee and—" He gave the waitress his most charming smile. Getting people to do what he wanted was, after all, his forte. "I'm looking for somebody to help me put on a roof."

She pointed at a booth. "Tim and Brent aren't doing anything."

He laughed. "I'm not looking for charity. I want people who could use some extra money."

She set a cup and saucer in front of him, and pointed again at the men. "Tim and Brent could both use some Christmas cash."

He picked up his coffee and walked to the booth, introducing himself. From working with superstar clients, he knew the best way to control a rumor was to start it, so he told them he was a friend of Elise McDermott who had inherited the McDermott farm and he was looking for help putting on a roof. Both took the information in stride, not really caring who needed the roof or why. Both were eager to get extra money for the holidays.

But Jared knew the waitress had heard and the news that Debbie McDermott had a granddaughter no one knew about would gradually wind its way through town.

He drank his coffee with Brent Logan and Tim Tibbadeau and they told him about a building supply store in the neighboring small town. Both accompanied him there to help him find the materials he needed. Everything was going incredibly well until Jared picked up a hammer.

He was suddenly transported back in time to law school. He could hear MacKenzie's voice welcoming him home after eight hours of construction work and four hours of night school, and almost smell the wonderful dinners she could create using the very little money they had because most of what he earned went for books and tuition.

"You never seen a hammer before?" Tim asked.

Jarred back to the present, Jared faced Tim and Brent, who looked equally confused by Jared's behavior. Luckily he had an excuse for standing there staring like an idiot. "No, I'm just not sure what kind of tools Elise will have at the house."

"I can't believe old Miz McDermott had a granddaughter," Tim said, chitchatting as he had been on the entire drive to the building supply store. A tall man with broad shoulders who wore a baseball cap to keep his hair out of his eyes, Tim was the happy-go-lucky high school football coach.

"Did you know her dad?"

"Not really. My dad did, though. I once heard him talking about how Bill ran off in his twenties. Never heard another peep from him." He shrugged. "Everybody guessed he was killed or something. Cause Miz McDermott never talked about him, either. I think he embarrassed her."

Jared faced him. "Is that so?"

"Oh, yeah. My daddy said the guy was a bum. He says if old Bill was alive, and he knew his mama had died, he'd be home for that property." He paused a second, as if piecing everything together in his head, then he smiled. "So this Elise gets that little farm all by herself?"

Jared nodded, stifling a smile. His plan to get Elise's presence out in the open and people's curiosity aroused was working already.

Tim whistled. "That's a sweet piece of property. Probably worth a bundle." He peered at Jared. "Hey, you two aren't an item, are you?"

Jared reached up for another hammer. "Nope." But red-hot jealousy shot through his veins when he realized the other side of his plan to get people out to Elise's farm to meet her. Men would be interested in her, and not just for her farm. One innocent, yet somehow still sexy smile from Elise and it would be all over for every unmarried guy in the county. And hiring Tim Tibbadeau to fix the roof probably meant the high school football coach would be the first to fall.

Another round of red-hot jealousy roared through his blood. He shook his head, telling himself to cool it. What was wrong with him? Elise was a single mom who needed a halfway decent guy in her life. Tim worked for the high school and was willing to do odd jobs for extra cash to buy Christmas gifts. A man didn't come any more stable than that. And if she found a good man here while she was fixing up the property, she'd settle in this little town and probably be welcomed like part of the family.

Jared stopped his thoughts. Glanced around. She

would be welcomed in this little town like family. The lawyer who looked like Santa Claus had greeted her with open arms. The general store owner was willing to "put out feelers" for whatever anybody needed. The waitress had been sweet as pie, even though Jared was a stranger. Tim and Brent had volunteered to help put on a roof even before Jared told them he'd pay them.

Elise didn't need to find a husband or even a boyfriend to stay in this town. She simply needed to get among these people and see how friendly they were. She might not get the brothers and sisters she'd so desperately wanted. But she'd get a family. A whole town of people who would fill the roles of brothers and sisters, cousins, aunts...somebody might even be like a mother or father to her.

Jared returned to Elise's grandmother's with a new plan. Though it was growing dark, he backed the SUV up to the old wooden garage. He, Tim and Brent began unloading the supplies they'd bought. He heard the front door open and assumed Elise was coming out and glanced behind him. Tim and Brent were busy stacking shingles. He didn't care if either one saw her, but now that his plan was to get her to consider living here, he wanted her to go into town, not have the residents to come to her. He wanted her to spend a little time with Pete at the general store, introduce herself to the waitress at the diner, so she could see how warm and welcoming these people were in their natural environment. He didn't want her meeting people in her garage when God only knew what she'd look like...

He turned to face her again and his breath froze in his chest. Dear God, she looked so damned cute. In still-warm North Carolina, the jeans and T-shirts she wore for traveling had been replaced by a tank top that revealed the beginning swell of her breasts and cut off denim shorts showed off her legs. Her long red hair floated around her like a cloud. Fresh faced and innocent, yet sexier than any of his superstar clients, she slowly approached him.

"Do you have the sales slip?"

The light from the garage made her pretty hair sparkle and picked up the dusting of freckles on her nose. Jared waged a valiant fight against his usual case of male appreciation, but it was no use. After several days on the road, he finally saw the obvious. He wasn't attracted to Elise because she was pretty. He was attracted to her because she was pretty and didn't know it. Or at least didn't act like she knew it. She was sweet, honest, innocent. Any normal man would be a bit dumbstruck in her presence. Especially when the warm night allowed her to wear clothes that teased him with a sample of all the skin he'd love to touch.

Telling himself to simmer down, he produced the sales slip from his shirt pocket, suddenly realizing it wasn't such a good idea for him to stay at the house with her. With her anger over his asking her lawyer about her family apparently gone, he was back to fighting a bunch of longings he had no right to feel.

Elise smiled. "Thanks. I'll write you a check." She looked at the bill of sale, then back up at him. "I'm surprised you're not arguing."

He wasn't arguing about the price of supplies

because he was footing the bill for the labor. "I'm not going to ruin a deal that works for me."

She shook her head. "Never met a guy who considered putting on a new roof to be a treat."

"It's not a treat. It's a good deed. I happen to need one."

"Thought you only did good deeds as penance or for money?"

He wasn't about to tell her he needed to do penance for the way his blood heated in her presence. He turned away and said, "I need this one to tell my parents, remember?"

She laughed and shook her head, leaving him, Tim and Brent to finish unloading his SUV. He made a second trip to the store to retrieve the balance of his supplies, then after unloading them he drove Tim and Brent back to the diner.

It was after eight when he finally got home. His muscles ached, but his chest ached a little more. He knew that once the men in this little town saw her, Elise would be inundated with requests for dates and guys offering to help her get the house ready for sale. Though it was wonderful for her, he hadn't realized how empty it would make him feel knowing that she'd soon forget all about him. But his jealousy was wrong. His sexual feelings were wrong.

He stifled both as he entered the kitchen. "I hope this house has hot water," he said as he closed the back door behind him.

But he stopped dead in his tracks. The place was immaculate. Elise had given the kitchen a good cleaning and the appliances, though old, sparkled. The dusty curtains had been washed. A red and white checkered tablecloth sat on the round kitchen table.

Something that smelled wonderful bubbled on the stove.

"What is that?"

She grinned. "Jambalaya. I figured since you were in the South we'd show you what we're all about. Good cooking and hospitality."

"You could have boiled an old shoe and I would be thrilled."

"So the jambalaya will really work for you then?" she asked with a laugh, sliding Molly into an old wooden high chair, obviously something she'd found in the house.

"How'd you get all this?" He pointed at the corn bread and butter that sat on the table, along with glasses of tea and a homemade cake.

"You left your cell phone so I called the store."

He tossed her a skeptical look. "You called Pete?"

She shrugged. "Old Pete told me he wasn't one to let a woman and her baby go hungry. But I think he really came to check me out. I didn't make much of a first impression when we stopped for milk."

His heart stuttered in his chest. Half with jealousy, half with pride. She was already making friends. He should have recognized that someone who'd basically been on her own since eighteen would take the news that she was alone a lot better than he'd taken the news that his very healthy wife was suddenly dead.

She turned away, busied herself with her cooking. "I also found clean sheets and fixed up the guest room for you. I didn't try to use the upstairs bathroom since you're so sure something is leaking, but the one down here works."

"Thanks." He glanced around. He should have told her right then and there that he couldn't stay at the house, but she was so happy after having been so upset that he couldn't do it.

Instead he said, "How do you have electricity?"

"When I called Mr. Collins last month to tell him I was coming home to fix up the house, he said he'd get the utilities turned on. He's actually the one who suggested I live here while I had the remodeling done." She turned to the stove again, and stirred her jambalaya. "Now, go wash up, I don't want my okra to turn to mush."

Jared left the kitchen and walked through the downstairs looking for the bathroom. Wanting to think about anything other than staying with Elise…alone…again…he inspected each room as he walked down the hall. All were furnished with pieces that looked like they had survived the Civil War, but all were sturdy, stable.

He found the clean bathroom and realized again that Elise had made very good use of her time while he had shopped for roof supplies. Wishing he had time for a shower and to change clothes, but absolutely fearful of mushy okra since he had no idea what that was, he only washed his face and hands and returned to the kitchen.

He walked to the table beside Molly who sat in her high chair. "Hey, Molly," he said to the baby before addressing Elise. "You could probably get big bucks for some of this furniture on the Internet." Glad to have found a safe topic of conversation, he added, "I have friends who can help you get set up."

"Maybe."

"There's no maybe about it. You could sell this furniture for a bundle."

She joined him at the table and reached for the bowl of fluffy white rice. She scooped three spoonfuls onto her plate then covered the rice with the soupy red jambalaya.

"I don't think so. I guess… I guess…I'd like some time with the furniture…to see if I can figure out who my grandmother was."

He raised an eyebrow. "You think you're going to get to know her from her furniture?"

She shrugged and took a piece of cornbread. "Maybe."

"The place was all but cleaned of personal effects." He frowned and glanced around. "I wonder who did that?"

"Because I had the same question, I also called Mr. Collins while you were gone." She peeked at him. "He told me that he had asked the church ladies who knew my grandmother to clean out her things in case he had to sell the place as administrator of her estate." She smiled at Jared. "It was his way of maintaining her privacy."

"Makes sense." But it didn't make him happy. She was capable, confident, able to find things out, get things done on her own. Without him. She didn't really need him. And if she didn't need him, he had no idea what he was doing in this house, eating with her, when technically his only place in her life now was as a roofer.

He cleared his throat, forcing away those odd thoughts. "Tim and Brent, the two guys I asked to help with the roof, both thought your grandmother was a nice lady."

She glanced around at the homey kitchen. "I'm guessing she was."

Love bloomed in her eyes as her gaze touched the curtains, the countertops, even the utilitarian appliances. Realizing that though she had the basics, there were still things she'd need, Jared recognized his place in her life had shifted from rescuer to idea man. She might not need somebody to get her out of trouble, but she did need somebody to get her on a good course and stay there.

"So once you have a few days to hang around with her things, start making an inventory. Like I said, I know people who can help you get set up on the web."

She laughed. "You're so insistent that I sell this stuff. How do you know I don't want to take some of it with me?"

It seemed the perfect time to ask her if she'd ever considered staying in this house. But he stopped himself. Though she'd obviously had a long conversation with Mr. Collins and had sweet-talked Pete into delivering her groceries, she hadn't yet seen enough of the town to realize how easily she would make friends, how easily the residents would accept her and probably care for her once they found out she had no family.

But he hadn't forgotten her stubborn streak and knew that it would be much better if she figured it out on her own.

"Just keep the Internet thing in mind."

She shook her head with a laugh. "Whatever."

"I'm serious."

She stared at him. "You're missing the point. This is all I have left of my family. I want their things around me."

Jared frowned down at his plate. He'd sold everything he had in New York because it brought painful memories of a woman who'd left him, not because she wanted to, but because she had died. Elise had found herself wanting to keep everything she had of her grandmother, the mother of the man who had deserted her, because the things comforted her.

But he and Elise had faced two totally different life traumas. She could bounce back, appreciate what was left behind for her, because she hadn't played a part in her torn and tangled life. He'd been the orchestrator of his misery. No man wanted to keep a sofa and chair, tablecloths and dishes, sheets and pillowcases that reminded him that he had been horribly, horribly wrong and it had cost him the very woman who had inspired him to be bold enough to take a risk.

He expertly shoved away any thought that had to do with MacKenzie's death, busying himself with taking a bite of his food. He groaned. "This is wonderful."

Elise brightened like the lights he'd seen on the Christmas trees in yards on his way home from the building supply. "I knew you'd like it."

"I love it."

"Great. You can do the dishes."

He laughed. "I don't like it that much." Molly pounded on her high-chair tray and he made a face at her causing her to giggle, all thoughts of his other life gone as if he'd never had them. They ate the rest of the dinner making companionable conversation about the cleaning Elise had done that day. When dinner was over Molly yawned, and he changed his mind about the dishes, volunteering to do them while Elise got Molly ready for bed. He knew he was stalling, delaying telling her that he would be staying in the bed-and-breakfast, but he convinced himself that helping her after she'd had such a hard day of work was just another kindness.

When she returned downstairs, he had the kitchen clean and the leftovers in the refrigerator.

"She went right to sleep."

"Do you have a crib?"

"An old one I found in the attic. Though I want to keep a lot of my grandmother's things, this crib is just about shot. I can make do with it for a few weeks, but eventually I'll have to replace it."

And that was it. That was all they had to talk about.

The kitchen became uncomfortably quiet and Jared glanced around again. He should go. Even if the bed-and-breakfast didn't have a room, all he had to do was get back on the interstate and find one of the hotels that were peppered along the highway to take advantage of weary travelers. Elise and Molly were settled and in no danger. Why couldn't he just say goodbye and go?

Elise casually said, "I get the bathroom first."

And Jared knew why he couldn't leave. She expected him to stay and he couldn't disappoint her. She might be moving on with her life, able to handle any task that came her way, but she hated disappointments. Life had handed her so many that she could no longer hide how much they hurt her. Even he'd delivered a near knockout punch when he'd ask Mr. Collins about her family. He couldn't hurt her anymore.

He put aside his own feelings, told himself he could handle one simple sexual attraction and said, "I forgot. We're back to one bathroom."

Elise didn't seem to care. "Yep. One bathroom and I called it."

On a triumphant laugh, she turned and left the kitchen, not even in the slightest concerned that they were sharing living quarters again. Proof that she was coming to trust him, not for help or money or even advice. She trusted *him*. Something she couldn't do just a few days ago when forced to share a hotel room in the storm.

Of course, they were in a house, a lot more space than a hotel room. But to Jared's hormones that didn't seem to matter. While she ran to her bedroom as if nothing were amiss, his eyes turned upward, as his ears picked up her footfalls above him, and his mind centered on the knowledge that she was gathering something to sleep in, probably sweet-smelling soaps and gels and about to get naked to shower.

Telling himself to stop being a damned fool, he ambled into the living room and turned on the TV. When he heard Elise leaving the bathroom, he let a few more minutes go by before he went upstairs. On his way to find Elise and ask where she'd stowed his duffel, he passed a room with a lamp lit, and glanced inside.

Elise stood at the crib, cooing to Molly. She turned when she heard him, and his stomach did a flip-flop. She wore a pretty pink robe over pink-and-white striped pajamas. The outfit was perfectly covering, but the color brought out the best in her complexion and made her look incredibly pretty. She didn't look young. She didn't look frightened or worried. Her life was straightening out and her burdens easing. Evidence of that shone very clearly in her face.

He licked his suddenly dry lips. "I just wanted to ask where you put my things."

She walked out into the hall with him, closing the door behind her. "Second door on the right." Holding his gaze, she added, "And thanks. I know you're doing this because you don't want to go home, but it's a big help to me."

He swallowed. She didn't look scared or nervous. She wasn't at his mercy. They were just two people, a man and a woman, standing in a dimly lit hall, alone. And he liked her. He liked her a lot. The attraction he felt for her wasn't just a case of his hormones awakening after five years of lying dormant. He *liked* her and wanted nothing more than to run his fingers through her thick, unruly hair, skim them along the slim line of her jaw, kiss her. Satisfy his curiosity about how sweet she was. Acknowledge the fact that after five long years he was suddenly coming back to life. And suddenly starving for female companionship.

But that was his side of the story. Hers was very different. She'd been abandoned by her dad, lost her mom and then left alone and pregnant by a man she'd obviously trusted. One way or another, this house would provide the first real stability in her life. She was getting a second chance. A chance to find out who she really was, what she really wanted, who she'd be if she didn't have the worry of money hanging over her head.

And if the way he'd lost his wife had taught him anything at all, it was that he didn't deserve a second chance. Let alone a second chance with somebody like Elise.

He took a breath and stepped back, away from her. "Good night, Elise."

CHAPTER SEVEN

THE next morning, Jared ambled to the coffeemaker with a casual, "Good morning," as if nothing had happened between them the night before. But Elise wasn't letting him get away with that. Everything he'd been thinking as he stood staring at her in the hall outside Molly's room had been in his eyes. She'd seen the hunger, the heat, the need. She didn't have any idea what they should do about it, but she did know they couldn't ignore it. They had to talk about it if they planned to live together while he fixed her roof.

"Good morning." She waited as he set his coffee on the table and then said, "There's cereal in the cupboard."

He gave her a long, slow look before turning away and her heart tripped over itself in her chest. The look he'd just given her reminded her that he could be experiencing nothing more than a case of close-proximity-inspired lust, an extension of what they'd experienced in the hotel room. But she didn't think so. Too much had happened the day before.

"I had Pete bring cereal and muffins, but I should probably run into town today for more food."

"Fine, but if I'm going to be eating here while I fix that roof, we should pay for the groceries equally."

She gaped at him. "You're putting an entire roof on my house. So, no. You don't help pay for the groceries."

For the first time since he walked into the kitchen, he caught her gaze. Something warm and syrupy flooded her system at the same time that Jared's eyes flickered and she finally understood. The spark they'd been fighting all along had morphed into something different. And that was what she'd read in his eyes the night before. The attraction wasn't just about sex anymore. They'd spent enough time together, done enough things together, poked in each other's lives enough that they liked each other. The only problem was he didn't seem pleased.

So she had a decision to make. Did she spend the few days they had together while he fixed the roof convincing him that what was between them was worth exploring? Did she even know if it was worth exploring? There was a great big swatch of his life she didn't know. She could spend the next few days flirting and teasing and getting him to open up to her, only to have him get in his SUV and head for New York, never to return.

After all, everyone in her life left her. There was no reason to believe he'd be any different.

At dusk, Elise walked out to her front yard as Brent, Tim and Jared climbed down the ladder. She offered everyone dinner, but Brent and Tim said they had to get home. Brent to his wife and four kids. Tim to an energetic hound who needed a long walk.

Though she recognized Tim would have liked to

stay and get acquainted, she was glad he had to go. She needed more information about Jared before she made any decisions about what she was feeling for him. Which meant she needed every second of her time with him. Preferably alone.

By the time Jared walked into the kitchen, dinner was ready to be served. Molly had been fed and sat in the high chair chewing her teething ring.

"I need to wash up."

She nodded and smiled brightly. "Okay."

Jared gave her a funny look. "Is something wrong?"

"No. Everything's fine."

He sighed. "I've been in the rescue business long enough to know that when somebody's denying some-thing a little too strongly or a little too happily that means there *is* something wrong."

"Go wash up."

"Okay. But we're talking when I get back."

Jared took longer than expected. When he arrived in the kitchen barefoot with wet hair, she knew he'd showered.

He winced. "Sorry, but I was filthy." He pulled out a kitchen chair. "I'd forgotten what a dirty job putting on a roof is."

She pulled out her own chair and sat. "That's okay. I appreciate you doing this."

He grabbed the platter of pork chops and took two. "That's why you're giving me the cold shoulder? Because you appreciate what I'm doing?"

"I'm not giving you the cold shoulder." Lord, she was trying so hard not to look obvious that she was giving him the wrong idea.

"Okay, if there's nothing on your mind, then there's something else we have to discuss."

She knew the tone and suspected he'd finally figured out a way to dismiss their attraction, so he was ready to talk about it. She could already hear the conversation in her head. He'd explain why it was a bad idea and follow up by telling her why they'd do nothing about it, but at least he wouldn't be denying it anymore.

"Oh, yeah?" She smiled smugly at him. "What do we have to discuss?"

He pulled in a breath. "I got a room at the bed-and-breakfast."

That knocked the haughty wind out of her sails. "What?"

"I can't stay here. This is a small town. I'll ruin your reputation."

There were so many things wrong with his reasoning that she didn't know what to say first. After several seconds of stunned silence, the only thing that came out was, "You drove me the whole way from Los Angeles, now you're putting an entire damned roof on for me and you won't let me thank you by keeping you for a few nights?"

"You saw what happened between us last night."

"Yes. I did. But we're adults. We've been dealing with this all along. We can handle it."

This time Jared looked down at his plate, refusing to meet her gaze.

But his not saying anything said everything. "You're not afraid that we'll do something we'll regret. You know you're leaving and you don't want to hurt me."

He looked up. "Is that so bad?"

She'd never had anybody like her so much he felt he had to leave. She could have exploded and reminded him that everybody who said they'd loved her had gone, that he was nothing special. But the two men who had left her, her dad and Patrick, clearly put themselves first. Jared wasn't running to save himself a bit of awkwardness. He was hurting himself to save her pain. How could she be angry with him for that?

"So you're refusing my hospitality...for me?"

He nodded. "I do this for a living, remember? I know how to keep people out of trouble."

"Did you call the bed-and-breakfast? Make sure they had a room?"

"When I came down from the roof for a glass of water this afternoon, I saw the cell phone on the counter and decided there was no better time to call and make a reservation. I'm booked for three nights."

Three nights. That meant he believed he'd need four days to finish her roof.

Staring into his serious gray eyes, in the quiet of the kitchen, Elise was suddenly tongue-tied. In four days he would be gone. But he liked her enough to protect her reputation—to not trust himself to be alone with her anymore. He might be leaving for the night, but he'd be back in the morning. Plus she now knew the strength of his feelings and she really did have a decision to make.

"Can I at least pay for the room?"

He shook his head tiredly. "I think we both know I can afford it."

"Yeah, but you're only staying in Four Corners because—"

"Because I'm helping a friend. A *friend*." He reached across the table and squeezed her hand. "For once, let it go, Elise."

She didn't remember him ever having said her name. At least she'd never heard him say it so intimately. It sounded smooth and sexy on his tongue. She tilted her head—their gazes still locked—and once again his eyes told the whole story. Need. Desire. Yearning so strong he couldn't even lie to himself anymore, let alone her.

He liked her.

He *liked* her.

She glanced down at their joined hands, then back at his face.

Suddenly it was all very real. Not just a fantasy she'd spun. Not just a sexual attraction. He *liked* her.

And he had a past he wouldn't talk about. Not to mention parents waiting for him in New York City. It didn't matter that she liked him, too, that part of her longed to explore what was happening between them. He had to go. That's why he didn't want to explore this himself. Their time together was only an interlude. Not something they should take seriously and certainly not something to risk a foolish mistake over.

She pulled her hand from beneath Jared's and licked her suddenly dry lips. "Okay. I get it."

He calmly reached for the mashed potatoes. "Looks like you've been cooking all day."

She took a shivery breath. His dismissing his feelings for her so casually felt like a betrayal. But it wasn't. All along they'd been attracted. All along she could easily see why she'd be drawn to him. He was a rich, brooding man who was so sexy he could make any woman's mouth water. But she was a poor single mom. Pretty on a good day. Frazzled most others.

If he liked her, it was only because of proximity. Once he got to New York, he'd find a woman more suited to him.

And maybe he knew that.

Maybe that was the real reason why he didn't want to explore these feelings that thrummed between them.

Jared didn't waste time after dinner. He helped with the dishes, but as Elise climbed the stairs to put Molly to bed, he walked to the front door. "I'll see you tomorrow."

She stopped and faced him. "You're going?"

"Yeah."

She looked as if she would argue, but instead pasted on a smile. "Okay. See you tomorrow."

Jared walked out the door into the surprisingly cool evening. With the warm sun beating down on the black roof, he'd been hot all day. The coolness caught him off guard, but also reminded him of why he was still in Four Corners, North Carolina. Someone he liked needed him. He was in his element. Helping someone else to forget himself.

Climbing into his SUV he realized that the extreme difference in the temperatures was a mirror of his life. When he was in the glare of the lights of one of his clients, the world was easy. He could say and do what needed to be said and done because he always had the answers for other people's problems. At night when he was alone, things were cold, hard, difficult. There might be books about grief, but no one could go through it for him. No one could talk him out of his sense of responsibility. No one could tell him it was okay that he'd gotten his wife killed.

And that's what he had to remember every time he looked in Elise's soft green eyes and wanted to drown in them. She didn't deserve to be drawn into his drama. Didn't need it. There were plenty of men in Four Corners—men without baggage—who would want her.

He drove to the bed-and-breakfast and was met by an elderly gentleman. "Welcome. My name's Dave. You must be Mr. Johnson."

"Yes," he said, putting his big suitcase on the floor. He'd long ago finished off the clothes he kept in the duffel for emergencies and needed the things in his second bag. Of course, if he could wash some things or buy some shirts and jeans better suited to putting on a roof that would be ideal.

"Is there a mall nearby where I could buy some jeans?"

"No need to travel that far. Pete's got jeans and work shirts, if that's what you're after."

"That's it exactly. How about somewhere I can wash a few things? Is there a Laundromat?"

Dave frowned. "I'm not sure." He brightened. "But it doesn't matter. We have a washer and dryer. You're welcome to them."

Jared smiled. He'd never been in a place so warm, reinforcing that Four Corners would be the perfect home for Elise and Molly. "Thank you. You know, your whole town is really something."

Dave glowed with pride. "We like to think so." He turned and called, "Aaron!" and a young boy—no older than twelve—appeared from a door at his right. "Take Mr. Johnson's bags to the Summer Retreat Room."

Aaron grinned and nodded, grabbing Jared's bag and heading up the steps.

Dave went behind a discreet desk. "I'll show you the washer and dryer once we get you settled. If you'll just sign in here and give me your credit card, I'll run it." He smiled at Jared as he handed him his credit card. "The Summer Retreat Room is a nice room. And you remember, anything you want, anything you need, you call. Maude and I pride ourselves on keeping our people comfortable."

Jared smiled, unexpectedly uneasy. This was what he was accustomed to. People waiting on him. People jumping to do his bidding. So why did it feel so strange tonight? Why would he rather be in the creaking old bed in the house that had leaky plumbing and needed a roof?

He told himself it was because he was worried that if something happened in the middle of the night, Elise would be alone, but he knew that wasn't true. Still, he also knew there was no way in hell he would do anything about what he was really feeling.

Elise awakened to a very cold house the next morning. The lower temperatures were closer to what she remembered from her childhood in North Carolina in December. The storm was getting closer and they might even have a white Christmas.

After dressing Molly and tossing on a pair of jeans and a T-shirt, she entered the upstairs hall and immediately smelled coffee. Realizing Jared had already arrived to work on the roof, she rushed downstairs and found him sitting at the table, reading the paper, a plate filled with pastry in front of him.

He pointed at the plate. "Have a Danish. You won't be sorry. That Maude can really bake."

She burst out laughing. He was the strangest man. Quiet, yet likable. Bossy, but capable. A hard man to get to know, but an easy man to be around.

"Hey, they like me. I swear they'd offer me half the house if they didn't have a nephew who fully intends to inherit everything."

She slid Molly into the high chair, and walked to the counter to get the box of baby cereal.

Jared rose. "I'm serious about the Danish. I'll feed Molly while you get a cup of coffee and eat one."

She pulled the cereal from the cupboard. Today she wasn't in the mood to argue about anything with Jared. She liked him. She had for a while. She'd only truly admitted it the day before, but she'd liked him for a lot longer than that. They had four days left together while he repaired her roof. And she wanted to spend them *with* him. Not in the house alone, while he worked on her roof. They might not have forever, but for a few days she'd like to bask in the glow of being with someone who truly cared about her.

She retrieved a bowl, poured in some fluffy flakes and said, "Get the milk from the fridge. I'll fix the cereal. Then you can feed her while I eat a Danish. And it better be as good as you claim if I'm wasting an entire morning's worth of calories on it."

"Oh, it is." He walked to the refrigerator and got the milk. He took it to the counter where she stood, and as he handed it to her their gazes caught and clung.

She wished she was prettier.

She wished she was older, smarter, or even simply sophisticated enough to be what he needed.

But she wasn't. She couldn't be. Otherwise, he wouldn't be sorry that he liked her. And he was sorry. She could see it in his stormy gray eyes. Still, she wanted her remaining days with him. *With* him. Not listening to him walk on the roof above her.

She put her attention on mixing Molly's cereal. "I sort of have a favor to ask."

"What?"

She took a breath. "I need a car."

"So call Pete. Get the name of a nearby dealer and take the SUV to shop for one."

She licked her lips. "You trust me to buy a car by myself?"

"Are you saying you can't?"

"It's just that I've never done it. It's going to be a huge chunk of my savings. So I don't want to make a mistake."

"I suppose Brent and Tim could work alone today."

"Really?"

He inclined his head, obviously thinking through the possibility and he smiled. "Yeah. Give me a few minutes to get them set up and then we'll go."

"Great! I'll shower and get dressed."

"I'll call Dave to get the name of the car dealer."

"Okay!" She raced out of the room. Her heart light. But halfway up the stairs she stopped. It was awfully darned easy to convince him to spend the day with her. If she were the hopeful type she'd think he wanted to spend time with her as much as she wanted to spend time with him. But she knew life a little too well to be so fanciful.

He was up to something. She could feel it in her bones. And she didn't necessarily think it was good.

CHAPTER EIGHT

AS SOON as she was gone, Jared pulled his cell phone from his pocket. He hit the memory button he'd pro-grammed for the bed-and-breakfast. If he was getting a few hours with Elise, he was going to make the most of them, introducing her to every damned person he could and showing her that Four Corners was the kind of town a single mom should settle down in.

"Four Corners Bed and Breakfast."

"Hey, David. It's Jared."

"Jared? Everything okay?"

"Yeah, except Elise needs a car. We're going car shopping this morning and it would really help out if you and Maude could look after her baby."

"Are you kidding!" David's voice spiked with awe. "We haven't had a baby here since the O'Haras stayed a few months back. We'd love a little one for a few hours."

"Great. By the way, where is the best place to buy a car?"

David gave him the name of and directions to Four Corners' used car lot, as well as the dealership in the neighboring town. Just as Jared finished the conversation, Elise returned to the kitchen wearing low-rise jeans, a little pink top and a gray sweatshirt.

She looked better than any woman Jared had ever seen. Her eyes held a wariness, but he'd become so accustomed to that that his brain skimmed right by it and focused on how sexy she was, how soft she looked, how much he'd just like to touch her. Just once.

He swallowed and forced his eyes away from her and his attention on their plans for the morning. "I called David. He gave me the name of the local car dealer. Four Corners only has a used car lot. If you want a newer car, he suggested we might want to try the dealership in Omega."

"I can't afford a new car."

"David said the dealership gets some really good cars as trades on new ones. He thinks you might like one of those better. He and Maude also agreed to watch Molly."

Her gaze drifted over to his. The wariness in her eyes had multiplied exponentially. "Oh."

He didn't like tricking her, and technically he wasn't. If he'd driven her to the bed-and-breakfast and dropped the bomb that they were leaving Molly, that would be trickery. But he was being forthright with her.

Still, a little sugar always helped the medicine go down, so he smiled before he said, "These are good people, Elise."

"But we're fine."

"I know. But look at this as an experiment."

"Experiment?"

"You're a single mom. Eventually you'll have to get a job." He stepped over, and automatically caught her hands the way he would with a wayward starlet. The softness of her skin amazed him, and could have made him forget what he wanted to say. He let them go, stepped away from her. "Someday you'll be leaving Molly in day care. Why not practice by leaving her with someone we like and trust."

"*You* like and trust."

"Fifteen minutes with Maude and David and you'll like and trust them, too."

He scooped Molly from the high chair and said, "Is she ready as is?"

Elise hesitated then sighed in resignation. "All right. You're right. I figured you were up to something when you agreed to help me so easily. But I see your point. I'm going to have to go back to work sometime and when I do, Molly will have to go to a sitter or in day care. So, leaving her with your friends is a good practice run. Let me wash her face. Then we can go."

They drove into town in silence. Nervous about leaving her baby with strangers, no matter how good an idea it was, Elise focused on the decorations. Red and green ornaments glistened in the sun, as silver and gold tinsel shimmered in the breeze that was bringing the impending storm.

Molly sat in the back of the SUV, chewing a teething ring, oblivious to the fact that for the first time since birth she would spend real time away from her mother. When Jared parked in the small lot behind the bed-and-breakfast, Elise got Molly before he could even think of carrying her into the house. If she didn't like the look of Maude and David, she wasn't leaving her baby with them.

They walked up the steps of a wraparound porch and Elise inhaled sharply. "If nothing else, I love their house."

"It's beautiful inside. Wait until you see it."

He opened the door for her and Elise stepped into the foyer. The curved oak stairway was decked out in silver tinsel and red bows. The small writing desk she assumed served to check in guests was trimmed in miniature white lights. But as they walked through the downstairs, winding through cozy sitting rooms and hallways, Elise saw that beneath the sparkle of Christmas decorations was sturdy wood furniture in a house decorated with practical elegance.

"Dave?" Jared called when they'd passed through several rooms without finding the owners.

"In the kitchen."

Jared pointed down a short hall and Elise walked forward. He pushed on a swinging door and led her into the kitchen.

The huge, modern kitchen surprised her. She hadn't expected to find stainless-steel appliances and granite countertops in a house so quaint. Beyond the cooking area was a long wooden table that had been painted black, surrounded by ten black and chrome chairs.

Obviously seeing her surprise, Dave winked. "Maude's gotta have somewhere to bake."

The short, slender gray-haired woman Elise guessed to be Maude slapped his arm. "*He* wanted the kitchen for his big, elaborate seafood dinners. Not only does he invite half the town, but he wants them all to be able to sit in the kitchen and talk while he's cooking."

Jared laughed. "Elise, this is Maude and Dave Greenway, owners of Four Corners Bed-and-Breakfast." He faced Maude and David. "And this is Elise McDermott. She inherited—"

"We know." Dave interrupted "She got Debbie McDermott's place." He pulled out one of the chairs in the eating area. "Give me the baby and you sit."

Protectively hugging Molly, Elise turned to Jared. "Do we have time to sit?"

"We have plenty of time. All day. The work Tim and Brent have to do today is basically laying shingles. It's slow and boring, but easy. They'll be fine without me."

Elise swallowed. Dave approached her, a wide smile on his face, a happy sparkle in his eyes.

But Elise shied away. "Let me take off her coat."

Dave stepped back. "Sure. I'll pour us some coffee."

He walked away and Elise began to feel foolish. She knew everybody was placating her. But this was her first time of leaving Molly. The only person who'd ever held her baby with any kind of regularity was Jared.

As she slid off Molly's coat, Jared reached for it. He also took the diaper bag from her shoulder. "I'll set these in the blue room."

"Oh, you mean the Tropical Paradise room?" Dave asked, as he brought four cups and a carafe of coffee to the table.

Jared sighed as if put upon. "Dave named all his rooms."

"All the big bed-and-breakfasts do that." He winked at Elise again. "I like to keep up with the competition."

She laughed and walked over to the table where Maude stood silently, watching Elise. As Elise approached, Maude pulled out her chair. "She's a beautiful baby."

"Thanks." Elise sat.

"Jared tells us you're a single mom."

"Yes."

"Then it's good that you got Debbie's place."

Elise took a breath. "Yes. I certainly need the money I'll make selling it."

David poured four cups of coffee and handed one to Elise. "That's going to bring you a pretty penny."

"I'm hoping."

"Or she could keep it," Maude put in. She turned to Elise. "That's a beautiful place when it's kept up. Such a lovely yard for a child. You might want to think about keeping it."

"Oh, I couldn't." She stopped, not wanting to reveal her whole life to strangers then wondered why not. She'd be gone in a few weeks. It didn't matter what she told them. "I need the money for a start in life."

Dave sat at the table across from her. Jared took the seat next to her. As Dave handed Jared's coffee to him, he said, "Why not sell a few acres off the back of the property as building lots. That'll give you a jumpstart."

Jared's eyes narrowed. "Just how big is that property?"

"About thirty acres. Not much in terms of a farm these days, but if you cut three acres off the back of that property and sell them to people wanting to build out in the country, you'll get a tidy sum and not lose your privacy."

Elise had never thought of that. "Really?"

"I could help you," Dave said. "I was in real estate before I took up this gig."

Elise took a breath. She'd have a home and money. Something so wonderful she almost couldn't wrap her mind around it. "I'll think about it."

"You have weeks until you get that property fit for a Realtor to see it," Jared put in casually as he stirred cream into his coffee. "Plenty of time to consider it."

Elise faced him. He wanted her to stay. It was written all over his face. "You're losing your touch as a rescuer."

"What?"

She laughed. "When we first started our trip, you were a lot better with getting me to do things without realizing you were manipulating me."

"Maneuvering you." He put his spoon down and over the rim of his cup his eyes met hers. "It's a subtle difference but an important one."

Elise's breath stuttered. He was gorgeous and he liked her enough that he was working to make sure she made the right choices. He *knew* her enough not to force ideas on her, but to let them happen naturally. Yet he wished he wasn't attracted to her, wished he didn't like her. And the only reason she could think of was that for as many things about her that he liked, he must also see things that he didn't.

The topic of her property died, and a new subject rose easily, naturally and Elise could see why Jared believed Maude and Dave were the perfect candidates to watch Molly while he and Elise car shopped. They spent the better part of an hour talking about Four Corners and when she was obviously comfortable with the older couple, Jared rose.

"We better get going."

Elise rose, too, satisfied that Maude and Dave would take good care of her baby. "Yeah. Molly's about ready for a nap."

"Crib's all set up in the Happy Family room."

Elise laughed. "You didn't really name a room the Happy Family room."

Maude rolled her eyes. "He did."

When they were finally walking along the wraparound porch, on their way to Jared's SUV, Elise said, "So…I like them."

"I knew you would."

"And Dave's idea of selling off back acreage and keeping the house sort of intrigues me."

"I knew it would."

"I said *sort of* intrigues me. I didn't say totally wowed me."

Jared laughed. "That's good enough. Life decisions aren't to be made in a few seconds. Or even a few hours. You should consider them carefully. I simply wanted you to see this option."

"Seen and noted," she said, walking to her side of the SUV. To her surprise, Jared followed. He reached for the door handle before she could grab it, opening the door for her. Like a gentleman.

She froze. No one. *No one* had ever done that courtly gesture for her. Stunned into silence, she slid onto the seat, unable to even meet his gaze as he closed the door for her.

As they pulled onto the car lot, a man dressed in a green sport coat and tan trousers walked out of a booth-like building that served as the office for Tomko's Used

Cars. Smooth Ed Tomko, owner of Tomko's Used Cars, introduced himself the second their feet were on terra firma. Once they explained Elise was looking for a car, he tried to talk her into an SUV like Jared's, but knowing her budget Elise wouldn't be pushed into something she couldn't afford. Instead she chose a little blue car, something that would be fuel efficient.

After a test drive, she signed the papers and had the money transferred from her California bank account electronically. Smooth Ed promised the car would be ready for her the next morning, after one last check by his service department to change all the fluids.

Happy that she'd finally have her own vehicle again, Elise slid her hand into the crook of Jared's elbow as they walked to his SUV. He'd talked her into a lot of things today. Maneuvered her into others. Now it was her turn. "How about I buy you lunch?"

"I thought you'd be eager to get back to the baby."

"We could call Maude and Dave and if Molly is fine, I'll buy you lunch."

He pulled his cell phone from his jacket pocket and handed it to her. "The bed-and-breakfast number is programmed in. Just hit star then four."

Hearing that Molly had awakened from her nap and was happily playing in the high chair while Maude baked Christmas cookies, Elise smiled. She asked if Maude could handle Molly for another hour and Maude easily agreed.

"Looks like we're on our own."

She hadn't meant for the comment to sound romantic, or flirty, but even she heard the light, breathy note in her voice. Jared instantly pulled away from her. He made a quick move to the SUV, making it appear he'd pulled away because he was close to the car, but she knew the truth. He didn't want to be romantic with her.

She told herself that was for the best as they drove to the center of town, found a parking space in front of the diner and seated themselves in a booth in the crowded restaurant. The waitress brought two cups of coffee with her as she approached her table, set them down with a smile and passed out menus.

"I'll be right back. Coffee's on the house if you want another drink with your lunch."

Elise studied her menu then laughed. "Spaghetti and meat sauce, not meatballs." She shook her head. "Reminds me of my mom." Tears unexpectedly filled her eyes. Her mom was the one person in her life whom she could miss. She hadn't chosen to die. She would have loved Molly. *She* should have been the one to baby-sit Elise's little girl.

She closed her menu. "I'm going to get the spaghetti."

"I virtually lived on spaghetti and meat sauce in law school." Jared also closed his menu. "I'm going to get that, too."

As he said the words, his face contorted as if he couldn't believe he'd said them.

Elise laughed. "Surprised you're ordering the cheapest thing on the menu?"

"No."

"Then why'd you grimace?"

He put his attention on the cover of the menu. "Law school was hard. Tuition and books were expensive. I didn't really have time to make enough money to go

to school *and* live on. So corners were cut. The spaghetti reminded me. That's all."

"One of the first things you told me was that you'd
been poor once."

He laughed. "Poor doesn't even describe it."

She waited for him to elaborate. When he didn't, she
felt as if she'd thrown away an opportunity by not
forcing him to say more. Still, his saying anything
about his past life was a proof of trust. Something
warm and happy bloomed inside her. He trusted her.
After nearly a week of her trusting him, he finally
trusted her.

Lunch passed in companionable conversation about
the town with Jared clearly campaigning to get her to
keep the house and sell a few lots for expenses until
she found a job. After leaving the diner, they spent
another hour with Dave and Maude at the bed-and-
breakfast. By the time they got home, it was after five.
Dusk had settled and residents had lit their Christmas
lights. Everything in Four Corners sparkled to life.

When they arrived home, her house was dark, and
for some reason or another that didn't seem right. It
was a house made to be lived in, loved. And she was
a person who needed to love. Maybe the real home she
yearned for wasn't a person, or even people, but this
piece of property. A house and land. Both of which had
belonged to a grandmother who would have wanted
her. She had roots. She belonged.

She handed Jared the container holding her leftover
lunch. "I know you're eager to get up to the roof to see
what Brent and Tim did today, but would you put this
away while I take her upstairs? It's early for her to go

to bed but you heard Maude say she didn't take an afternoon nap."

He took the box from Elise's hand, but instead of turning away he leaned in and kissed Molly's cheek.

"Good night, sweetie."

Elise gazed at him, a lump in her throat. Jared was such a naturally loving person, it seemed odd that he could hold back so much of himself. So far he'd only trusted her enough to tell her he'd been so poor he'd eaten spaghetti through law school. Though he still had parents, and maybe even family, he was more alone than she was. And maybe he was the person who should be staying in this house, living in this wonderful town. Or maybe they should live together.

She turned away so he wouldn't see any of that in her eyes. "I won't be long."

Upstairs, Elise changed Molly and laid her in the crib she'd pulled into her grandmother's old bedroom.

When she'd arrived in the house, the beds had been stripped, the mattresses aired. The church ladies had cleared out most of Elise's grandmother's belongings, sending the clothes and personal items to charity. But she had linens and dishes, furniture and fixtures.

As she waited for Molly to fall asleep, Elise walked around the room, grateful for the jumpstart in life her grandmother had given her. Running her fingers along the dresser that she'd polished the day before, she wondered why she couldn't just be happy with her good fortune. Why she was so intent on drawing Jared into the picture?

Patrick had fooled her into believing he was misunderstood. A guy who had never gotten a break. He was young, good-looking, naturally brilliant and filled with big plans. To an eighteen-year-old, he had seemed like a man with so much potential. And now here she was seeing Jared the same way. Not that she believed Jared was irresponsible, as Patrick was. She knew he wasn't. It was more that she'd seen Patrick as somebody who needed love, and now here she was seeing Jared like that, too quickly giving him the benefit of the doubt. She really didn't know why Jared didn't want to go to New York City. Because he kept delaying the trip she presumed he had something to face. Something he refused to talk about.

But what if she was all wrong, as she had been about Patrick? What if Jared simply didn't want to go home? What if he didn't like his parents?

Why was she reading so much into this? Hadn't she learned her lesson about assuming the best about people who didn't deserve it? About trusting people who didn't deserve to be trusted? She didn't know Jared well enough to assume anything good or bad. Yet, she'd more than given him the benefit of the doubt. She was worried about him. And maybe she shouldn't be.

After peeking at Molly and seeing she was asleep, Elise walked downstairs and found Jared standing by the door, ready to leave.

She took a breath. "Thought you were going to check on things on the roof?"

"It's too dark to go up." His hand on the doorknob as if dying to leave, he added, "But I could see that Brent and Tim remembered to put on the tarps. No matter what comes our way tonight, you'll be warm and dry."

"Good."

She couldn't think of a reason to make him stay, but she definitely didn't want him to leave. Theirs was the most confusing situation. She liked him enough that she worried about his future. He liked her enough that he couldn't resist looking out for her, that he was willing to wear scruffy clothes, fix her roof, when anybody else would have been long gone.

To a woman who was always alone, that was very sexy, as appealing as his dark hair that had been ruffled during the few minutes spent outside checking on the tarp. The guy who never wore anything but suits in California stood in the kitchen of an old farmhouse wearing a T-shirt, leather jacket and scruffy jeans. Looking so damned good, so damned tempting that her pulse jumped. Just once she'd like to touch him. Maybe kiss him. Just once.

Elise walked to him, expecting him to quickly twist the knob, open the door and leave with a brusque goodbye. Instead he licked his lips. "Well, I've gotta go."

Elise heard his words, understood what he was saying, but found herself mesmerized by his mouth. His lush, full lips. The curiosity of what kissing him would be like.

"You know, men take a lot of flak for staring at women's breasts when they talk, so I'm wondering if I should be offended that you're staring at my mouth."

She swallowed, raising her gaze until she met his, absolutely positive everything she felt for him shone in her eyes.

He groaned. "Please don't like me."

"I do." Feeling bold, knowing there'd never be another chance like this, she added, "And you like me, too."

"It's wrong."

She shrugged. "Sometimes that's just the way it is."

His silence could have chipped away at her courage, but the fact that he stayed at her door, not making any sort of move to leave, bolstered it. She stood on her tiptoes, slid her fingers to his shoulders, feeling the soft leather of his jacket beneath their tips, and lightly brushed her lips across his.

He sucked in a breath. One of his hands landed on the curve of her hip.

Her lips still on his, she smiled against his mouth, but just when she would have pressed her lips a little harder, he jerked away from her.

He stared into her eyes for a few seconds then he squeezed his eyes shut and took a hard breath. He said, "Good night, Elise," and was out the door before she could stop him.

CHAPTER NINE

ELISE awakened the next morning to the sounds of Molly's sobs. Tossing back the covers, she jumped out of bed. "Oh, honey, Mama's sorry! I didn't mean to sleep so late."

Sitting in the crib, tears wetting her cheeks, Molly held up her little hands, begging her mom to take her. Elise reached in and pulled her out, cuddling her close before she laid her on the bed. "Let's change your diaper then get you a bottle."

Molly's crying slowed to sniffles, as if she understood that now that her mom was awake, everything would be okay.

Walking to the dresser for a clean diaper, Elise mumbled, "This is what I get for kissing him. Not only did I toss and turn all night, but I slept through my own baby's crying. On top of that, things will be awkward when he gets here to work on the roof."

Still, she couldn't stop the smile that spread across her face when she remembered kissing Jared, remembered how he hadn't pulled away initially and how he couldn't resist lifting his hand to her hip. Chills tumbled through her. Her chest tightened with anticipation.

Things might be awkward between them, but he could no longer deny that he liked her. And she couldn't deny that she liked him. Maybe it was worth a little discomfort to get that out in the open.

She dressed Molly, rushed to get herself dressed and was still breathing funny when Jared opened the kitchen door. She turned from the counter where she was brewing coffee and their eyes met across the quiet room.

Her breathing completely stopped.

Wearing a flannel shirt and jeans, he looked so sexy and so male she could have swooned. She felt a fleeting sense of trepidation, wondering how she could hope a guy like him would be interested in a woman like her. Then she remembered the kiss.

He had wanted her as much as she had wanted him.

"Good morning."

She swallowed. "Good morning."

"You and I need to have a chat."

Of course. Another chat. But this time she wasn't going to let him railroad her. This time she had a few points of her own to make.

"Coffee will be ready in a minute. And I saved two of Maude's Danish—"

"She made French toast with apricot syrup for breakfast." He smiled ruefully. "So the good news is you can have both Danish. The bad news is I'm going to be as fat as a barrel if I don't soon get your roof fixed and leave."

The word "leave" caused her breath to shiver in her chest again. Her gaze swung to his.

He looked away, scraping a chair from beneath the table. "Sit."

Sucking in a long draught of air, she took the chair he'd pulled out.

He sat across from her. "Don't go spinning fantasies about me."

She rolled her eyes. "You have such an ego."

"Ego has nothing to do with it. Any fool would have felt the emotion in that kiss yesterday."

"And this fool did. That kiss made it perfectly clear that I don't feel any stronger for you than you feel for me."

Picking up the salt shaker, he leaned back in his chair. Before he spoke he dropped his gaze to the crystal container as if he couldn't look at her anymore. "That's what makes it so wrong."

"I don't think so. In the real world, all that emotion is what makes it right."

He glanced over at her. "I don't live in the real world, remember?"

"Maybe it's time you rejoined us."

"You don't even know me."

"With the possible exception of Michael Feeney. I think I know you better than anybody in the world right now."

He shoved his chair out and rose from the table. "Right. You don't even know that I was married." He turned and walked to the kitchen door. "So much for knowing me better than anybody in the world right now."

He closed the door behind him with a firm click and Elise sat in the silent kitchen until the coffeemaker groaned and Molly screeched, pounding her teething ring on the high-chair tray, asking for breakfast.

Numb, feeling like an idiot for not realizing a

gorgeous man like him had been married, she stood. Of course, he'd been married.

"I'm coming, Molly." She walked to the cupboard and grabbed the baby cereal, then retrieved the milk from the refrigerator. She prepared Molly's breakfast, poured herself a cup of coffee and took both to the kitchen table, seating herself in the chair next to the high chair.

If she didn't know something important about Jared like the fact that he'd been married, then she couldn't say for sure that he had feelings her. After all, what happened between them the night before was as much sexual as it was emotional. What she felt from him might have been nothing but a little lust—which would be wrong to him. Hadn't he said he didn't mess around with women who had babies? Plus, she wasn't as pretty as the women in his life. She wasn't educated or sophisticated. There was no way she could compete with the women he saw on a daily basis.

She squeezed her eyes shut. What an idiot she was.

How could she ever think he liked her?

Lust after her? Yes.

Like her? Not hardly.

Only a desperate woman, or the world's absolute worst judge of character, would think that.

And hadn't she already proven herself to be an incredibly poor judge of character?

Jared came into the kitchen at noon and walked through, directly to the bathroom to wash up. Standing at the stove, stirring leftover jambalaya, Elise didn't even turn around. The table had been set. A bowl by the centerpiece contained steaming white rice and drinks were already at their place settings.

Jared came out of the bathroom drying his hands. She said, "Aren't Tim and Brent coming down for lunch?"

"We're done for the day."

She turned. "What?"

"Tim and Brent both have other jobs. They've taken all the leave they had. Tomorrow they've gotta go back to work. So they had things to attend to this afternoon."

"What about the storm?"

"There's no reason to panic. Because there were three of us, we worked pretty fast and there's not a lot left to do. I can handle the rest alone."

"So that's good?"

"Exactly."

She thought about that for a second, and said, "Except without help, what would have taken another day will take two."

"Maybe three." He smiled sheepishly. Elise's heart turned over. How could she possibly stay angry or even distant with him when he looked like that.

"So I figured I'd take you to town for your car. Then you could drive yourself home."

Her chest tightened. "You're not having lunch?"

"Once we get your car, I'll grab something in town. But I'll be back to do some more work after that."

She swallowed her disappointment. They'd had such a good time the day before that he didn't want to risk any more time with her. "I hope you've at least called your parents and told them that your plans keep changing."

"I have." He caught her gaze. "They're fine. They just want me to be there by Christmas Day."

That was four days away. One day to drive and three days to work. Just as he'd said. What was really happening here was he was avoiding spending any more time than what he had to in New York.

He shrugged. "I'm hoping I'll be there on time."

"Liar." She shook her head. "You're hoping you'll find something else to delay you."

"All right. Maybe parts of me are." He focused his attention on grabbing his jacket. "There are a lot of memories I don't want to face there."

And suddenly she realized why he didn't want to go home. He didn't want to see his ex-wife. Maybe because he still loved her. She nearly groaned at her stupidity, at her naiveté.

"Anyway, grab Molly and we'll go get your car." Shrugging into his jacket, he walked to the door. "I'll see you in the SUV."

Elise stood alone in her quiet kitchen, telling herself she'd better get used to this and just as quickly telling herself that once she had her own car she didn't have to stay in her house and be alone. She could go into town. Maybe do some shopping. Maybe take Molly to the general store to visit Pete.

And suddenly she understood why Jared wanted her to stay in Four Corners and why he wasn't spending any time with her. He was forcing her into town. Forcing her to make friends. Without him.

That afternoon after Jared left her in town, she drove to Pete's to buy groceries, including a whole chicken. He might be forcing her to spend time in town, to realize it would be a good place for her to settle down.

He might even still be in love with his ex-wife. But she liked him. She enjoyed his company. She wanted to part on good terms, maybe have a few good memories of the one person in life who'd helped her without expecting anything in return. She wasn't going to let him deny her the few days she had left with him. If she had to guilt him into eating supper with her by preparing something that took extra time and effort, something he couldn't refuse, then that's what she'd do.

She raced home, put away her purchases and immediately stuffed the chicken. By the time Jared came off the roof for supper, her house smelled like heaven. The roasting chicken not only scented the air; it also warmed the kitchen.

"Yum," Jared said, closing the door behind him. "Something smells wonderful."

"Wash up. Everything will be ready when you are."

"Elise, I should—"

"You should stay and eat. I got hungry and I roasted a whole chicken. I can't eat it alone." She caught his gaze. "Besides, I put a lot of effort into this, trying to repay at least a little bit of your kindness. You wouldn't want to disappoint me, would you?"

The barb hit its mark. Jared shook his head in dismay, but strode back to the bathroom and stripped off his shirt, which was filthy. He washed his face and arms, but as he turned to grab the towel he caught his reflection in the mirror above the sink. His hair poked out in all directions. His face had a healthy glow he hadn't seen in years. His eyes sparkled.

He licked his suddenly dry lips. He knew why. He also knew why he was dragging his feet on the roof. At first he hadn't wanted to go to New York. Now he didn't want to leave North Carolina.

He wasn't entirely sure how it had happened, but he did believe Maude and Dave were to blame. Had he been forced to stay at Elise's, he might have concluded proximity caused the sparks between him and Elise. But he was staying at a quaint and cozy bed-and-breakfast, with a woman who could be the world's greatest cook, yet he still counted the minutes until he arrived at this little house and saw Elise and Molly.

He scrubbed the towel across his face, growling at himself. *This was just plain wrong.* He had to settle his past. He didn't have a future. At least not one that included a woman. He couldn't let himself fall in love with her. Not to save himself, but to save her. So she wouldn't be hurt when he left.

But every damned minute he spent in her company it got harder and harder to deny what he wanted to feel for her.

He walked to the kitchen, saw the stuffed chicken on the simple wooden table in the old-fashioned kitchen and was transported back in time to his parents' house. Pulling out his chair, he suddenly understood his dad. He'd loved his life. He'd loved working hard, coming home to Jared's mom, the woman who loved and supported him. Their lives had been simple, but honest.

And maybe that was the appeal he now saw in Elise. A simpler, more honest life?

Stop. Even if that's it, you don't get a choice. You had your happiness. You ruined it. You ruined it.

"Chicken, mashed potatoes, green beans," Elise said proudly as she took her seat at the table.

He stared at the food. All his favorites. The meal MacKenzie had made the day he passed the bar. "You need to stop being nice to me."

"You're putting a roof on my house." She smiled. "I'm allowed to be nice." She turned to the high chair at which Molly sat. "You get to eat some big people food today."

The baby giggled.

But he kept his gaze on Elise. She might be carrying on simple, easy, normal conversation, but her face glowed. He knew the look. Knew what she felt. But instead of talking about what was really on her mind, she pretended everything was okay.

"Molly loves mashed potatoes."

Jared slapped his fork on the table. "Would you please stop behaving as if there's nothing going on between us?"

"There *is* nothing going on between us. You won't let anything happen between us. Remember?"

"And you won't let it alone! You keep hoping and pushing! That's why you made my favorite dinner!"

She laughed. "This is your favorite dinner?" She shook her head. "If I made your favorite things, I did it accidentally."

"Accidentally?" He pointed at the green beans as if they'd done something offensive. "You got it right down to the green beans!"

She gaped at him. "How the hell am I supposed to

know your favorite dinner when you've never told me? Hell, Jared, even you reminded me this morning that I don't know you!"

Memories of the day he'd passed the bar poured through him. In his head he could hear MacKenzie's voice, her laugh when he called to give her the good news. He could smell the special dinner she'd made for him, feel the excitement that bubbled in his blood as he bounded up the apartment stairs to tell her he could keep his job in the D.A.'s office.

The scene suddenly morphed and he still smelled the chicken but he was walking out of an elevator into a cleaner, well kept corridor to the new apartment they could afford two years later. He could see himself opening the door, inhaling the scent of his favorite dinner, racing inside eager to see the woman he adored…and finding her in a pool of blood.

He bounced out of his seat. "You wanna know about me? Fine. Here it is. My parents were blue collar. They lived in a house something like this one." He looked around, seeing the similarities in the two kitchens, feeling the pull back to the past again. "They wanted me to have something better, so they scrimped and saved so I didn't have to go into debt to get my degree. But law school was expensive and I had to be on my own."

"Jared, stop."

"Oh, no. You wanted to know…I'm going to tell you. I'm going to tell you that I met a girl two months before I entered law school and fell in love so hard I couldn't wait to finish before I married her. We lived like church mice until I passed the bar. But she didn't mind. Oh, no. She wasn't the kind to mind."

Elise rose from the table. "If you're not going to eat," she said quietly, "I'm going to put this away."

"What? Suddenly you don't want to know?" He grabbed her arm. "All this time you've done everything from drop hints to out-and-out ask about my past. Now, I'm telling you and you don't want to know?"

She took a breath then met his gaze. "Not this way. Not when you're angry."

"Don't rob me of the one honest emotion I have!"

"Anger might be honest, but it's never the right emotion."

"Oh, and what should I feel when I come from work one night and find my wife dead? Should I be happy?" He tightened his grip. "Especially considering it was my fault. I might as well have pulled the trigger when I bragged to the press that I was about to bring down Tommy Hernandez. Some A.D.A. I was. Tough on crime. Yeah. Right. Crime was a little harder on me than I was on it."

He watched the color drain from Elise's face and realized what he'd done. Dropping her arm, he turned away. "I've gotta go."

She didn't argue. Didn't say anything and Jared didn't blame her. From the look on her face he'd say he was finally getting what he wanted. Her mistrust. There was no way in hell she'd like him anymore.

CHAPTER TEN

THE next morning, Jared arrived an hour later than usual, and after the sounds of his SUV door slamming, Elise heard him climbing the ladder to the roof.

Her heart ached for him. Not only had his wife been murdered, but he blamed himself. He hurt so much the pain of the loss radiated from him as he spoke, permeated his words. There was nothing she could say or do. Certainly not anything that might make him feel better. Twelve hours of being away from each other hadn't changed that.

So Elise fed Molly as she drank a cup of coffee and ate some toast. While Molly happily played with some brightly colored toys on her high-chair tray, she tidied the kitchen.

The knock at the back door surprised her and she turned from the sink just in time to see Maude walk in. "Hello?"

"Maude! What are you doing here? Shouldn't you be at the bed-and-breakfast?"

"Oh, Dave can handle things on his own. He likes it when I'm gone." She removed her coat. "I thought you might want some time to go shopping on your own." After dropping her coat to a hook by the door she lifted Molly from the high chair. "Some time to buy gifts for you know who."

Elise laughed. "You can come right out and say things in front of her. I don't think she really gets the whole deal about Santa yet."

"Oh, you'd be surprised what babies know." She kissed Molly. "Now, you run along."

Elise bit her lower lip. "Actually I'd like a few minutes to talk with Jared alone before I go, if you don't mind."

Maude busied herself straightening Molly's bib. "Sure. Go ahead. We're fine."

"Thanks."

Elise retrieved her gray fleece jacket from the hook by the door, walked out of the house and climbed the ladder to the roof. "Hey, this looks great."

Jared didn't take his eyes off the shingle he was sliding into place. He looked worn and tired as if he hadn't slept the night before, and Elise's heart ached for him.

"I'm not going to talk about it."

"Of course you are. You have to. But if you like we can start off by talking about the weather." She finished the climb and slid onto the roof. "Sheesh. It's cold."

"There are no trees or buildings to provide protection. So it just feels colder."

"Makes sense." She glanced around. "Peaceful up here."

"That, too."

He didn't say anything more, concentrating on his work. Two shingles were placed before Elise finally said, "You know, since Maude is here I can sit up here all day."

"No, you can't. You'd hate wasting that much time."

She shook her head. "Wow. You really do know me."

"You're easy to read."

"And now that I know a few things about you, you're easy to read, too."

He said nothing.

"You are. That whole penance thing you had going? That was all about the guilt you feel over your wife's death."

"Let it alone, Elise."

"No. I have a feeling I'm the first person you've ever told about your wife. That means one of two things. Either you trust me. Or it's time."

He peered at her. "Time?"

"Time for you to talk about it."

"You don't want to be annoying me when I have a nail gun in my hand."

She laughed. "That's the Jared I know."

"I thought we already established that you don't know me."

"We were wrong. The addition of those few facts you told me last night put the whole puzzle together. I think I know you pretty well now."

"Great."

The sarcasm in his voice made her laugh, but she quickly sobered. "I'm sorry for you, Jared."

"Don't be."

"Anybody who heard your story would hurt for you, but Jared, it's time to let go. To forgive yourself."

He put his head back and looked at the sky, then blew his breath out on a slow sigh. "You're not going to drop this are you?"

"No, so you might as well tell me why you won't forgive yourself."

He closed his eyes. "I want to. But I can't."

"I think you can. Actually I think you *are* forgiving yourself. And that's the problem. The proof of that is that you like me. Being with me makes you want things you've told yourself for the past five years you weren't entitled to. So every time you take a step, make a move, you remind yourself of the past and you stop."

She waited until he looked over at her before she said, "Your wife's death must have been awful. And I can see why you'd feel responsible. But there's nothing you can do to change any of it. It's over now. It's time to move on. I'm even guessing your wife wouldn't want you to suffer anymore."

He laid the shingle in place and hit it with the nail gun.

Elise hugged her jacket around her. "Was she pretty?"

"Who?"

"Your wife."

At first she didn't think he'd answer, but finally he said, "Yes. Very pretty. A blue-eyed blonde."

She whistled. "Top of the line."

He chuckled and Elise's heart stopped. Laughing was a good thing.

"She really was top-of-the-line. Pretty. Smart. Kind. Sweet."

"Sounds like a really nice woman." And he could talk about her in a good way. But he couldn't take those final steps. He couldn't get beyond the grief because he felt he didn't deserve to be forgiven. That's why he stopped himself every time he wanted to touch her or kiss her…or even share an intimate conversation.

But Elise couldn't help him with any of that. The final choice to move on had to be his, and if he didn't make it before he left, she'd lose him forever.

"So how much longer?"

He glanced over at her. "How much longer till what?"

"Till the roof is done."

"Two days."

Two days. Just as he'd planned all along, he'd leave her on Christmas Eve. The very last day that he could leave.

And he'd never call because he believed he was being gallant by leaving her. Never even think of her because he didn't believe he was allowed.

She pressed her lips together to keep them from trembling then quietly said, "Maude's watching Molly so I'm going into town to buy her a Christmas present."

He didn't look at her. "Okay."

She swallowed hard. He was back in the shell and this time she didn't think he was coming out again. "Okay."

Jared watched her scoot to the edge of the roof, then climb down the ladder. Long after she was gone, he stared after her.

All this time he'd been trying to get her to trust him and the unthinkable had happened. *He* trusted *her*. He couldn't treat her as if she were meaningless to him. She wasn't. He had no idea how he should treat her, but it could no longer be as if he meant something to her but she hadn't had any effect on him.

She affected him more than anybody had in five years.

He couldn't pretend that hadn't happened.

He also couldn't pretend he didn't want her. That kiss the night before had nearly been his undoing. Five years of being all but celibate had made him hungry and Elise was like a feast. He wanted her so much that he couldn't help wondering if that wasn't really the problem. Maybe he didn't like her as much as he simply wanted to sleep with her?

Elise returned from shopping with bags of toys for Molly and a paper sack of fast-food hamburgers enough for her and Jared in case he decided to stay for dinner. She didn't think he would, but she couldn't help wishful thinking.

The gathering storm clouds seemed to get thicker by the hour. The temperature had plummeted. She ran up the porch steps, the wind pushing her along, and rushed into the house. The door slammed closed behind her. Jared walked into the foyer, holding a happy Molly.

"Dave called for Maude to come home. I think he missed her."

"Oh. I'm sorry!"

"Not a problem. I was done on the roof for the day. And perfectly happy to fill in."

She dropped the bags and reached for Molly. "Hey, baby. Your mom is home."

Jared held her away from him. "I'm okay with her. Take your packages upstairs."

She displayed the sack of fast food. "Hungry?"

"I made a casserole."

She gaped at him. *He was staying for dinner? And he'd made it?* "You made a casserole? With what?"

"I took the leftover chicken from last night and threw it together with noodles and a cheese sauce."

Not at all sure what was happening, she smiled. "Sounds wonderful."

"Don't praise before you taste." He turned toward the kitchen. "Put your things away."

Elise ran upstairs and tossed the toys she'd purchased for Molly onto the bed. When she entered the kitchen, Molly sat in her high chair, chewing her teething ring, as Jared set the table.

"You're certainly handy to have around the house."

"Storm's coming."

She didn't have to be a genius to realize he'd deliberately changed the subject. She had no idea why he was here, no idea why he'd cooked her dinner. She only knew she wasn't risking this time by pushing him about anything. She walked to the refrigerator and pulled out the iced tea.

"The wind's a pretty good indicator that the storm's just about here."

"I don't feel right about leaving you tonight."

Ah, that was it. The rescuer was back. "I have a car."

He glanced over at her. "If something happens you'll come to the bed-and-breakfast?"

"And disturb an entire house full of guests? I don't think so. Besides, what's going to happen?"

He ran his hand along the back of his neck. "I don't know."

She laughed and sat at her place.

He sat, too. "I'll leave my cell phone for you."

"Okay."

He took her plate and dished on a serving of his

cheesy noodle casserole. "You are getting a phone eventually, right?"

"I have to."

"How did you manage to exist all this time without one?"

"I had a cell phone. Patrick took it when he left." She deliberately scooped up a bite of casserole and stuck it in her mouth so she wouldn't have to say any more about Patrick because she didn't want to. Patrick was so far in her past that she didn't even think about him anymore. Didn't want to. Didn't want to dwell on a mistake.

She savored the delicious bite then said, "This is wonderful."

"Thanks. A little recipe my mom taught me."

It was the second time he'd offered a casual tidbit about his parents, but when he didn't elaborate, she put her attention back on her cheesy noodles and uncomplicated conversation. "I'm guessing the storm will keep you from working tomorrow?"

"Probably. But while Molly was napping I took a trip up to the attic to check out the roof from underneath, and I found a box of Christmas decorations."

She peered over. "Oh, yeah?"

"Lots of outdoor lights." He cleared his throat. "If you want, I could put those up for you before I go."

She took a breath, refusing to meet his gaze. She wanted him to stay because he wanted to stay. He only wanted to make sure she had a nice holiday. Still, there was no way she'd miss even a minute with him.

She raised her eyes, caught his gaze. "Yes." She took a breath. "Yes, I would like help putting up the lights."

Elise told him how her mother had trimmed the

outline of the porch roof of their house with Christmas lights and he agreed that would be a good idea, very festive. He told her stories of living in Brooklyn, fighting his way through the crowds of shoppers to get lunch during the holidays.

They cleared the table and washed the dishes like a husband and wife, sharing the events of their days as they cleaned the kitchen.

But when the work was through and Elise suggested a game of rummy, he shook his head. "No. I should get back."

"I'll get your coat." Disappointed, she turned to walk to the foyer closet. Carrying his coat into the kitchen, she pasted on a brave smile.

Handing his leather jacket to him, she said, "You really should have something heavier than this."

He took the coat from her and bobbed it up and down as if testing its weight. "Yeah. Living in L.A. the past five years, I've forgotten how cold cold really is. This won't cut it in New York."

She swallowed. "Yeah. It won't." Disappointment rattled through her. She couldn't believe he was leaving her. With every fiber of her being she knew they belonged together, but if he couldn't see it, couldn't let go of his past, couldn't forgive himself, then what difference did her feelings make? He wouldn't stay. And if she continued to let herself spin fantasies, when he left she wouldn't just be alone; she'd be alone and miserable.

She struggled to pull herself together as she said, "Good night," and breezily turned from the door.

But his hand shot out and caught her waist, spinning

her around again. In one fluid movement, he pulled her to him and lowered his mouth to hers.

Her heart stopped. Her breathing stopped. Nothing existed but the feeling of his warm lips on hers. A thousand sensations tumbled through her. A thousand thoughts competed for attention. But one amazing reality pulled itself to the forefront. He couldn't leave without kissing her. He couldn't help himself.

She slid her hands up the front of his jacket, feeling his muscles tighten beneath her fingers, as his whole body went rigid. She thought he would pull away. Instead he growled against her mouth, hauling her closer and kissing her deeply.

The world spun for Elise. She and Patrick had been little more than inexperienced teenagers when they met. After a few years their kisses had become complacent. But Jared knew how to kiss. He knew how to coax her to him. He knew how to tease her into wanting more. He knew how to make her nerve endings crackle with anticipation, and her heart race with wicked yearning.

Just as quickly as the kiss started, he ended it. He pulled away and looked into her eyes. She couldn't speak. Could barely breathe. If a simple kiss could make her blood heat and her knees weak with desire, what would happen if they became lovers?

He pulled in a breath, turned and opened the door. "Good night, Elise."

The door closed before she could whisper, "Good night, Jared." But she was glad it had. She had some thinking to do.

CHAPTER ELEVEN

THE next morning Jared awakened to a winter wonderland. As the weatherman had predicted, the storm had finally found them. Three inches of fluffy snow coated the ground like thick, white frosting on gingerbread.

He stared at it for several minutes, his eyes steady on the elegant world around him. He'd forgotten how much he liked snow, the crisp feel of the air in the winter. The hushed, solemn mood after the year's first real storm. The clean, unblemished look of snow without as much as a single footprint.

It cleared a man's head. Brought him face-to-face with the truth. Caused him to see things that might otherwise be obscured by the noise of everyday life.

A few minutes later, he ambled into the dining room. Dave sat at the long table.

"May I use your phone?"

One of Dave's furry white brows lifted. "City boy like you don't have a cell phone?"

"I have one. I left it with Elise. I didn't want her alone with the baby with the storm coming."

"Good thinking." He pointed toward the side door.

"There's a phone in the sitting room. You can have some privacy."

"Thanks."

In the sitting room, Jared lowered himself to a red velvet Queen Anne chair, lifted the receiver and took a breath. Though he was calling his own cell phone, jittery nerves tightened his stomach muscles. Part of him felt like a teenager, finally venturing to call the girl he'd had a crush on all through high school. Another part of him felt like a man who desperately wanted to sleep with the woman he desired. The kiss hadn't done a damn thing to alleviate his need. If anything, it had heightened it—a cue that his physical feelings for her would only grow stronger.

He dialed his cell phone number and waited three rings before Elise answered. "Hello?"

"Hey, it's me."

A pause. "Hey." Her voice was soft and breathy, so feminine everything masculine in Jared awoke. He'd also forgotten how wonderful it felt to have a female in his life. Someone who fit with him. Someone he wanted to touch and taste and feel naked against him.

"I just wanted to make sure you and Molly were okay."

"We're fine. Are you having breakfast?"

"Just about to."

"What did Maude make for you today?"

He closed his eyes and sniffed the air. "I think it's omelets."

"Wow."

"I could bring you one."

She laughed. "Right. As if the whole town doesn't

wonder about me already. I can't have you bringing me breakfast from Maude every day."

"The whole town doesn't wonder about you anymore. They've already met you and know you're goofy."

She laughed. He smiled. He'd also forgotten how much he liked to make someone laugh.

He swallowed. He'd forgotten so much and was remembering it all so quickly. Maybe too quickly. And maybe for all the wrong reasons. He'd been celibate most of the time since MacKenzie's death. The few affairs he'd had had been brief and simply for sex. What he felt for Elise went beyond that. It tangled feelings and sex and thoughts of tomorrow and he hadn't had any of those in five years.

Wasn't a hundred percent sure he was ready for it.

Didn't want to hurt her if he wasn't.

And he would hurt her if he initiated something then ran in fear.

He cleared his throat. "The other reason I called was to tell you that I won't be out to the house this morning."

"Oh?"

"I know I promised to help put up the Christmas lights. And I will. I'll be out this afternoon."

"Okay. What will you do this morning?"

"I thought I'd take in the sights."

"The sights?" She giggled with glee. "What sights?"

He smiled at her confusion. "You might not realize it because you grew up in a little town like this, but Four Corners is quaint and interesting. I just figure that since I'm here, I could take a look around, maybe buy a camera, get some pictures and have something to talk about with my parents."

"Okay."

"So I'll see you this afternoon."

She paused just long enough for Jared to wonder if she was about to tell him not to bother coming that afternoon. She had to realize he might not be ready for what was happening between them. She had to know he could hurt her. She was a smart woman who would recognize that she should protect herself.

She said, "I'll see you this afternoon," and Jared let out the breath he'd been holding. He didn't know what they'd talk about for an entire afternoon. Didn't believe it was a good idea to get involved with her. But he couldn't simply fix her roof and run. He owed her something. He didn't exactly know what. Maybe he'd figure it out that afternoon.

"Okay. I'll be by around two or so."

He ate breakfast with Dave, getting the scoop on the tourist attractions in town. Before heading out on his sightseeing tour, he walked to Pete's store where he'd purchased the work boots and shirts he wore to repair Elise's roof, and bought a throwaway camera and a heavy coat. Shoving his hands deep into the pockets, he ambled along Main Street, feeling like himself—a fully alive, fully awake version of himself—for the first time in years.

He sucked in a breath of the crisp December air and soaked in the ambiance of the little town decorated for Christmas, clearing his head to get his bearings. He was a thirty-four-year-old man with millions of dollars and a law degree, who had passed the bar in two states. Logically he could assume that with a little study he could pass the bar in any state, which meant he could go anywhere he wanted, be anything he wanted. And the only thing he really wanted was Elise.

But that was wrong. She was eight years younger than he was, settling in a little town with a simple life. He'd never been simple. He'd always been complicated. A workaholic. Even if he gathered his courage and stayed with Elise, when the first client called and drew him back to L.A., he'd return to work and forget all about her because that's what he did.

At least that's what he'd done to MacKenzie. He'd gotten lost in his work. He'd left her alone so much that the few memories he had of their last days together were of him leaving the apartment or returning home after a long day's work. And that's what he'd do to Elise. Except he'd leave her in North Carolina while he was gallivanting through L.A. And that's *really* why he couldn't let anything happen between them.

MacKenzie's murder, his grief, Elise's own troubles were only a smokescreen for the real issue. He was a workaholic. And just as MacKenzie had deserved better, so did Elise.

After several hours of perusing little shops and visiting historical landmarks, he ambled back toward the bed-and-breakfast to shower before he drove to Elise's. Walking by the jewelry store, a wink of gold caught his eye and he stopped.

A gold heart.

He tilted his head studying it. He didn't know why but for some reason or another it reminded him of Elise. He tried to remember if he'd seen her wearing one, but couldn't think of a time that she had. After a few seconds he realized the heart made him think of

Elise because she'd helped him fix his. He might have hardly spoken, but that was part of why she'd been the perfect person to be with when he was coming out of his haze of grief. She listened. She'd only pushed when necessary. She'd done all the right things.

He glanced at the sign in the window that said, The Perfect Gifts For The Perfect Person For Christmas and decided it *was* the perfect gift for Christmas. He had to leave before the actual holiday, and he wouldn't be coming back. But he couldn't leave without giving her something. It might not be wise to want her to remember him, but somehow it seemed right.

The sun had been out for several hours by the time Jared drove to Elise's, so though yards and fields were still covered in white, the roads were dry in most places. He maneuvered down the long lane to her house, his tires crunching on the cold gravel. Recognizing Maude's car in the driveway, he nearly turned around without going inside. But he took a breath and parked the car. He would hurt Elise enough when he left. He wouldn't disappoint her the few times they had left.

But he also wouldn't give her a gift in front of Maude and create expectations that wouldn't come true. So he stuffed the little jewelry box in his jacket pocket, then zipped it closed so it didn't accidentally fall out.

Elise opened the front door before he knocked. "Merry Christmas!" she greeted gaily, as she opened her home to him.

He stepped in, stomping snow from his work boots.

Maude entered the foyer, carrying Molly. "Merry Christmas."

Jared shrugged out of his jacket. "What has you two so festive?"

Elise beamed at him. "We're baking cookies. Want one?"

She directed him to hang his coat on the foyer coat tree. He tossed it on with a soft plop, and as he pulled away, his arm slid up and toward her. But he jerked it to a stop and yanked it back. Elise tilted her head in question. Had he just fought the instinct to pull her to him for a quick kiss hello?

She tingled at the thought that he so naturally, so easily wanted to kiss her.

"I'm not much of a cookie guy anymore," he said, following Maude into the kitchen.

Elise scrambled behind them to catch up. As she entered the doorway, Jared stopped at the table. He picked up one of the icing-painted Santa cookies and smiled. "Fancy."

Maude laughed. "Painting cookies is sort of a family tradition. Dave and I get very creative with our icing."

Elise handed a church-shaped cookie to him. "I even painted the stained-glass windows."

He laughed. "MacKenzie sprinkled sugar cookies with red and green sugar because that's all we could afford." He shook his head and Elise held her breath. He'd never told her his wife's name, but it was obvious that was who he was talking about. She watched his face, looking for signs of pain but he only glanced at Maude and said, "MacKenzie was my wife. She died."

Elise suppressed a giant sigh of relief at his calm explanation, as Maude said, "Oh, I'm sorry."

He smiled sadly. "It was a long time ago." He glanced at the table filled with cookies again. "So did you make gingerbread?"

"Those were next on our list."

He frowned at the table laden with all shapes and sizes of painted sugar cookies. "You're making more?"

"We'll probably bake away the rest of the afternoon," Maude said with a laugh. "Dave's got my kitchen filled with shrimp. He's having some fishing buddies over for poker and he's making them a small feast."

"Oh. Elise and I were planning to put up the Christmas lights. Since I have to get back to the roof tomorrow, this might be our only chance to get those decorations up."

Maude clapped her hands together. "That's a great idea. Molly and I will be fine."

Grateful for both something to do and a reason to get him to herself, Elise headed for the door. "Give me a minute to put on a coat."

She raced through the hall to the foyer confident, but nerves jangled through her as she ran up the steps and into her room. With Molly, private time with anybody was a premium. But she suddenly realized that after two kisses, private time with Jared had new meaning. They were finally taking real steps toward acting out their feelings for each other. Would he kiss her again? Did she want him to?

The answer came quickly, easily, and made her breathless. Yes. Yes. She wanted him to kiss her as many times as he could before he had to leave her. She didn't care that he probably wasn't coming back. She didn't care that he had another life. One she didn't fit into. If this was their only time together she wanted to make the best of it.

When she returned to the kitchen, Jared was already outside. She walked onto the back porch and heard rumbling noises coming from the garage.

He came out, carrying the ladder. "I had to get this first."

She sidled up to him with a smile. "Where are the lights?"

He all but jumped at her nearness, increasing the speed of his steps. "Shoot." He leaned the ladder against the wall. "I left them in the front hall closet."

"I'll get them."

"I'll get them."

She caught his arm and stopped him. Smiling, she said, "We can get them together."

He wouldn't meet her gaze. Instead he headed for the steps. "Okay."

Elise sighed. Their time together wouldn't be any fun with him so distant and afraid. On impulse, she reached down, grabbed a handful of snow, quickly formed it into a ball and tossed it at him. With a re-sounding thump, it hit him squarely in the back.

He stopped dead in his tracks, and turned to face her, a shoked expression on his face. "What the hell was that for?"

She bent and scooped up another handful of snow, tossing it at him before he knew what was happening. This one hit him in the stomach.

"Elise, I'm warning you. Don't go there. I grew up in Brooklyn where snowball fighting is an art."

She ducked, grabbed more snow and threw it at him.

He scrambled down the steps. "So that's how it's going to be, huh?" He bent and tossed a snowball at her so quickly she didn't realize it was coming.

It caught her in the butt and she squealed with laughter, dipping to gather more snow. But before she could straighten again, he was in front of her pummeling her with snow.

She gasped and inhaled a mouthful of sparkling, wet crystals. Unable to breathe, she squealed, "Stop!"

He laughed. "I told you not to start something you couldn't finish."

But rather than concede defeat, she used his pause to bend again, scoop up a handful of snow and toss it directly into his face.

His expression was so incredulous that Elise roared with laughter.

"Oh, this is war now."

Before she could bob down to gather more snow, Jared plowed toward her, catching her around the waist. He hit her with enough force that she lost her balance and they both tumbled to the ground.

She managed one squeak on the way down, but when they landed with a thump, her in the blanket of soft white snow, him on top of her, her laughter stopped. The world around them hushed. The only sound was the rasp of their breathing.

He squeezed his eyes shut. "Why can't this last?"

"Why does it have to end when we make each other so happy?"

"Life, marriage—" he opened his eyes "—is about so much more than being happy."

"Do you think I don't know that? Patrick and I might not have made it official, but we were supposed to be a team. He never held up his end of the deal. This time I would like to be with somebody who will."

He rolled off her, staring at the sky. "Be with somebody." He shook his head. "You're so young that even the way you say things is different from the way I do."

"What would you say?"

"I'd say, 'this time when I have a relationship.'"

She giggled. "And that's different because?"

He caught her wrist, pulling her gaze to his. "Because when you say you want to be with me I think of sex. I think of warm covers and naked bodies."

She sat up and lightly brushed her lips across his. "Then I like the way you think."

He groaned. "You're killing me."

"Why? Because I like you? Because I think of you sexually? Or because I'm not afraid to admit it?"

"Because the thing you don't know but which would come out if we ever took this further is that I'm not made for a relationship. I'm a workaholic."

She cocked her head. "You think I haven't already figured that out? You forget you've told me more than once that you're on-call 24/7." She shook her head. "I can handle it. I'm twenty-six. Not nineteen."

With that, she kissed him again. His hands drifted to her waist, as his mouth came to life slowly under hers. He kissed her so gently that Elise would have never guessed he wanted her sexually, until the pressure of his mouth increased just before he reversed their arrangement. Rolling her into the cool snow, he deepened the kiss, opening her lips with his tongue. His hand slid along the outline of her sleek winter jacket and he groaned.

"You're wearing way too many clothes."

She opened her eyes. "So are you."

"So maybe we should take that as a sign?"

She laughed. "Especially, with Maude standing in my kitchen. Maybe even watching from the window."

His face twisted with horror. "Damn."

"Yeah."

He rolled off her and she sprang to her feet, brushing snow off her bottom.

"I'll get the lights."

She let him jog to the porch and even run up the steps before she stopped him. "Jared?"

He turned.

"*I'm* not afraid. I can handle anything you can dish out. I want to try."

"You don't know what you're saying."

"I do. *I'm* not afraid."

CHAPTER TWELVE

She hadn't meant for her words to sound like an ultimatum, but from Jared's silence as they strung the lights around the porch roof, she wondered if he hadn't taken them that way. When he left with Maude, rather than stay behind for more time with her and Molly, she could see in his eyes that he didn't really want to go. Yet he still left. She'd all but told him she was ready for anything with him, so the doubts he had were about himself. Whether or not he was ready for what they both wanted.

Maybe he didn't understand she'd fallen in love with him. Or maybe he didn't realize he'd also fallen in love with her.

Her breath oozed out on a slow, shivery stream. It was the first time she'd admitted that she loved him. The first time she'd been bold enough to admit to herself that she knew he loved her, too. Both admissions made her freeze with fear. Not because she was afraid of love. She welcomed it. What she feared was being left.

And Jared was leaving. Having a commitment to be in New York City with his parents for Christmas gave him the perfect opportunity to run from the very thing he most needed. To stay. With her. And risk his heart. While he was in New York, facing all the reminders of his past, of his guilt, he'd convince himself she'd be better off without him.

He wouldn't come back.

She ate a quiet dinner of a peanut butter sandwich and hot cocoa as she fed Molly a jar of baby food, wondering if he'd gone to the diner for his supper, and if he had, if he'd flirted with Destiny, the pretty waitress who worked the night shift. The thought of him with another woman filled her with teeth-gnashing jealousy and she suddenly realized she couldn't let him leave. No. That wasn't it. She had to let him leave. She couldn't be so cruel as to stop him from going home to his parents who hadn't seen him in five years. But she could delay his trip long enough to show him they had something special, something wonderful, something worth risking both their hearts for, and if he didn't come back she wouldn't be better off. She'd be alone. Again.

She absolutely would not let that happen.

With only minutes before Pete's eight o'clock closing time, she quickly packed Molly into her car and raced to the general store.

"I need a Christmas tree."

"A Christmas tree? Can you fit a tree in that little car of yours?" the older man asked with a disbelieving chuckle.

"I was going to ask if it could be delivered." She grimaced. "Before seven tomorrow morning?"

"Seven tomorrow morning?" This time his laugh was more genuine. "You're plotting something, aren't you?"

"Just trying to give Jared a Christmas surprise. I'm going to decorate the house and make a special Christmas Eve dinner while he's finishing up the roof."

Pete's voice softened. "That's a nice idea. He told me he's had some real tragedies in his life but he's going home for Christmas for the first time in five years."

Elise took a breath. The fact that Jared could now speak so openly about his past was proof positive he had moved beyond it. Before she and Molly came into his life, he couldn't even hold a polite conversation. Now, he wasn't merely talking about his life, he was making friends in the town Elise had made her new home. He loved them. She *knew* it. But she also realized that if she didn't make him see it before he left, he wouldn't come back.

"So can you have a tree at my house before seven?"

Pete laughed. "I love to be part of Christmas Eve surprises. My grandson Chase will be by with it first thing in the morning."

"Thanks, Pete. I just need a few more things."

Pete relaxed against the counter. "Take your time. I'm in no hurry."

She found the groceries she'd also need for her dinner, purchased them and left the store with a satisfied smile.

At home she immediately put Molly to bed then raced up to the attic to scout out the remainder of her grandmother's Christmas decorations, which Jared had discovered inspecting the roof. She found boxes of beautiful antique decorations and from the colors and style of the ornaments for the tree she knew her grandmother had been a lover of all things Victorian. She hauled them to the living room, knowing Jared probably wouldn't go any further than the kitchen when he arrived in the morning, but covered them with an old blanket just in case.

As prepared as she could be for the work she could only do once the tree had arrived, she walked to the downstairs bathroom to get ready for bed.

Stepping out of her jeans, she saw a blue bruise on her thigh and smiled. She didn't think she'd come out of the snowball battle unscathed, but she had won. Snowball fighting might be an art in Brooklyn, but in North Carolina it was more like war and she was a take-no-prisoners kind of fighter.

Stepping under the spray of the shower she closed her eyes and let the feelings from the afternoon pour through her again. When she caught Jared off guard, he could be the funniest, most fun-loving guy. He liked to joke. He liked to have fun. She couldn't believe he'd spent five years in mourning.

She also couldn't remember the last time she and Patrick had simply had fun together. She wasn't even sure they ever had. He was a brooding, angry young man when they left North Carolina together. His passion came from the bitter feud he had with the world.

Jared's passion came from— Well, if she was reading him right, his passion came from wanting her.

Wanting her.

Her.

Falling in love with her.

Having someone so attracted to her filled her with unspeakable joy. All she ever wanted was somebody who loved her for her. Somebody who stayed.

Though Jared couldn't stay, he would come back, if she gave him a strong memory. Something so powerful it would carry him through the difficult days he'd spend in New York. Something so powerful that he couldn't deny the obvious. She loved him and he loved her, and they should become a family.

And there was nothing so wonderful, so magical, as a baby's first Christmas. Jared might not get Christmas morning with them, but he'd see Molly's first look at the tree. He'd see the wonder in her eyes. He'd see the happiness on her own face as she finally had the means to provide a real home for her baby. And he'd know he had a place with them. A home. If things got difficult in New York, he'd think of them. And when his time with his parents was done, he'd come home.

Jared arrived late the next morning and didn't stop in the kitchen, not even to say hello. Elise took a breath, looking up at the ceiling, listening to his footfalls as he walked across the roof, knowing she was right. She had probably scared him silly the day before with her declaration that she wasn't afraid, but also realizing that he had to get on the road today. He promised his parents he'd be home for Christmas and if he didn't leave before noon he wouldn't get there on time.

Shoving those thoughts aside, she fed Molly, played with her a bit then put her down for a nap. While the baby slept she cleaned and dusted ornaments and decorated the tree Chase had not only brought to her house, but had also set up in her living room. She wound tinsel around the banister in the front foyer and topped it off with red ribbons. She prepared cider punch that made the whole kitchen smell like cinnamon, a pot of homemade vegetable soup and two loaves of crusty white bread.

When Molly awakened, she dressed her in a red velvet dress that had been a gift from a friend in California, showered herself and put on jeans and her best red sweater.

At noon, she walked out of her house, across the back porch and far enough into her yard that she could see on the roof. Shielding her eyes from the sun, she called, "Hey, I've got homemade soup if you're interested."

He appeared at the peak created by the meeting of the two roof halves, the blue sky his backdrop. "What kind of soup?"

She laughed. "Vegetable. But, seriously, when somebody offers you homemade soup, it shouldn't matter what kind it is."

He laughed, too. "No. I suppose not."

"Then get your behind down here and let me feed you lunch."

He hesitated, but said, "Yes, ma'am."

With the scent of homemade bread, bubbling soup and cinnamon punch wafting through the air, the kitchen couldn't have smelled more like home. As he walked in the door, Jared glanced around at the table covered in a shiny red cloth and decorated with a bowl filled with colorful Christmas tree ornaments as a centerpiece, and Elise held her breath.

"This is—" He swallowed. "Pretty."

"Wait until you see the tree."

"You got a tree?"

She nodded. "Pete's grandson brought it out and

set it up. I decorated it. And I also put Molly's presents under it. So you can be around for Molly's first Christmas."

He stared at her for a few seconds, then closed his eyes. When he opened them, the gray orbs were serious, solemn.

"Elise, I'm done. I have to get on the road. I shouldn't even take the time to eat lunch."

At first her heart skipped a beat, but her common sense kicked in. All she wanted was an hour. One hour so he would have a memory that he couldn't erase. One hour of feeling love for her and from her that would get him through the rough times in New York.

She grabbed a dish towel to dry her hands. "Okay, we'll skip lunch. Just watch Molly open a present or two."

"No. It's time for me to go." He walked a little farther into the room. "I know you're trying to show me that when I'm with you everything's okay." He drew in a sharp breath. "But I already know it. I'd be blind not to see that I'm different with you. But it doesn't change what I have to face. It doesn't change what I did all those years ago."

"Jared…"

He shook his head. "No." He headed for the door again. "I have to go."

His curt words cut her to the quick. A man who loved her wouldn't be that cut-and-dried. Emotion would have jumped in his voice at some point. But none had.

Tears filled her eyes. He liked her. He liked her town. He liked the home she could make for him, but he didn't love her.

And she wanted somebody to love her.

Her. Just as she was. Just for herself.

After a few seconds she felt his fingers on her shoulders. He gently turned her around. He lowered his
head and kissed her softly and Elise felt emotion vi-
brating through him. He tried to show her with a kiss
that she meant more to him than words could say, but
she knew the signs of a man conflicted. A man who
knew he had to go and couldn't come back.

Pulling away, he took his hands from her shoulders
and stuffed them in his jacket pockets as if not
wanting to risk touching her again for fear he wouldn't
be able to stop.

Toying with something in his pocket, he quietly
said, "I'm sorry."

He pivoted and walked to the kitchen door, opening
it without a backward glance. Within a few seconds she
heard his SUV engine start and the crunch of the gravel
as he drove down her lane.

Then silence.

Not wanting to think about Elise alone and upset, Jared
flew out of Four Corners and got on the highway that
would take him to the interstate. Still driving like a bat
out of hell, he reached it in record time. When he pulled
up the entrance ramp and saw the road was empty, he
wondered why he was speeding. It was Christmas Eve.
Most people were with families by now. He'd called
his parents early that morning and told them he would
be late. There was no point in hurrying.

He slowed down, and realized that without driving
to keep him occupied, he thought of Elise. He thought
of her soft skin, sweet kisses and the way she joked

about everything, making being with her fun. If he'd stayed as she wanted him to, tonight would have been the night he made love to her.

Yearning blossomed in him like a wild rose. He liked her so much, wanted her so much he sometimes almost couldn't control it. He was lucky to leave when he did. *She* was lucky he left when he did.

Needing to occupy his mind, he pulled his cell phone from his pocket and turned it on. It beeped and belched and pinged with voice mail alerts and text message announcements.

He winced. Holidays always brought out the worst in his clients.

Still, if he wanted to get rid of images of Elise standing in her warm kitchen in her pretty red sweater, hoping to celebrate Christmas Eve with him, his clients would bring him back to planet earth. His real planet earth. The world he belonged in.

He began reading the text messages. Brianna James had been photographed coming out of a bar totally drunk. Jared groaned. Deciding he'd deal with the fallout from that when he got to L.A., since he'd already missed most of the fanfare, he moved to the next message. Art Winfield was in a standoff with his studio on contract negotiations and he wanted somebody to hold his hand. Jared rolled his eyes. These people had big, beautiful houses. They had enough money for anything they wanted. They had staffs of hundreds of people ready, willing and able to keep them company while they waited for a studio to come to terms. Why did they always have to call him?

His clients had absolutely no idea how the real world ran because it had been so long since they'd been in it. Elise wouldn't whine if a studio took too long. She most certainly wouldn't go to a bar when she was in a bad phase of her career.

He took a breath. No. When life dealt Elise a bad hand she'd made the best of it. When Patrick left her alone and pregnant, she'd figured out a way to not just support herself, but also to stash a bit of money away. When she'd arrived in Four Corners, she'd forced herself to go into the town and make friends. She'd comforted *him* when she realized he was in a bad way emotionally. When she decided she wanted a real Christmas for herself, for her baby, for *him* she'd simply pulled one together…

And he'd left her.

He squeezed his eyes shut, then remembering he was driving, popped them open again. He hadn't left Elise alone. He'd left her with a town full of people. She deserved a chance to find herself—

That wasn't true. She knew who she was. She was comfortable, happy, confident in spite of a life filled with people leaving her.

Even he'd left her.

Her image flashed into his brain. The disappointed look on her face when he told her that he couldn't stay to watch Molly open her presents haunted him. His heart trembled.

He'd done the thing everyone in her life had done. Her dad had left her. Her mom didn't leave on purpose, but she'd died. Patrick had left. Now, Jared had left.

Everybody left her.

He was the one who longed to stay with her. No, he *ached* to stay with her. *He was the one.*

Yet, he had to go.

Didn't he?

Didn't he need to face his past?

Elise blew her nose and told herself to stop crying. It was Christmas Eve. She had a baby. She loved Jared with every fiber of her being, but he wasn't coming back and she had to get over it. She had to make Christmas special for her daughter.

She turned from the front door where she'd stood staring at her lane, hoping Jared would change his mind, and headed for the stairway. She'd allowed herself one long hour to hope, but hope was gone now.

Carrying Molly up the steps, she said, "We're going to take this dress off and put you in something comfy so you can take a nap."

Molly gurgled at her and Elise hugged her tightly. She always thought of herself as alone, but with Molly she really wasn't.

She took her baby upstairs, slid her into comfortable pajamas, sang her a lullaby and returned to the kitchen. The soup and bread were now cold. The punch was warm. The sweet scents of her special lunch mocked her. She was an idiot to think one lunch, one special Christmas Eve lunch, could get him to see that he loved her. Especially since he didn't.

She turned on the radio hoping to fill her mind with anything but thoughts of how foolish she was. When Christmas carols filled the air, she nearly turned them off, but she remembered that's what Jared had done on the first day of their trip and she deliberately left them on. She had to get beyond this.

With the carols wafting through her kitchen, she couldn't be sure but she thought she heard the sound of a car in her driveway. Deciding that was more wishful thinking, she turned on the spigot and filled the basin with soapy water. Another sound caught her attention, and she paused, absolutely positive she heard a door closing.

Telling herself to stop or she'd be insane before Easter, she filled the soapy water with the plates from the table.

Just as she would have turned to gather the soup ladle and knives, the kitchen door burst open and Jared plowed inside. "I'm sorry."

Elise blinked, half believing he was a mirage. "What?"

Closing the door, he drew in a long breath and quietly said, "I'm sorry."

She stared at him, still not convinced he wasn't a figment of her imagination. "You're sorry?"

He stepped a little further into the room. "You made a special Christmas Eve lunch and I didn't even taste the soup."

"You came back for *soup*?"

He pointed at the table. "Soup and bread." He met her gaze. "And Molly's first Christmas."

Her heart stopped. Her breathing stopped. Tears filled her eyes. *He was back.* "You have to go to New York."

He took a breath and another step closer to her. "I will."

Knowing how hard this was for him, and willing to meet him halfway, she took a step toward him. "Christmas will be over."

"We'll celebrate New Year's with them." He took another step.

She matched it. "We'll?"

"You and me, and Molly." This time he didn't have to stop his arm when it swung out to catch her around her waist. He didn't have to worry what she'd think when he pulled her to him. He knew she'd think exactly what he wanted to convey. "I love you."

Elise squeezed him so hard he felt all the pain she'd experienced in the short hour he was gone. He grabbed her shoulders and held her an arm's distance away. "I'll never leave again."

"Really?"

He held her gaze, wanting her to know she could believe him. "I promise."

"What about all those high-powered types in L.A.? What are they going to do without you?"

He pulled his cell phone from his pocket and clicked it off. "It's a funny thing. They did awfully well without me while I was gone, so maybe they don't need me so much after all?"

Her eyes that had been pooled with tears, suddenly filled with hope. "You're going to desert them?"

"I'm going to promote my assistant to a general manager position in my corporation and let her be everybody's go-to girl."

She smiled. "Go-to girl?"

"She likes titles."

Elise laughed. "Sounds like a plan."

"Actually," he said, slipping his arms around her again, "I had another plan."

He whispered his idea in her ear and she giggled with glee. "I like the way you think."

"So you've said."

"Molly's napping."

His grin widened before he lowered his head and kissed her. The scents of cinnamon, soup and fresh pine swirled around them and he knew he'd always associate Christmas with loving her. He'd said a private goodbye to MacKenzie in the car on the return trip to Elise's and came to this kitchen door a new man. Ready for whatever life had in store for them.

EPILOGUE

Christmas Morning!

IT SEEMED like only minutes had gone by when Elise was awakened by Molly's soft cries. It was finally Christmas morning. She opened her eyes expecting to see Jared beside her, but he was gone. Which was fine. She knew he was an early riser and expected to find him downstairs. Hopefully making breakfast.

She jumped out of bed. "Oh, Molly! It's Christmas! Let's go see what Santa left under the tree."

She pulled Molly from the crib, changed her diaper and ran down the steps. At the doorway to the living room, she pointed at the tree. "Look!"

The lights twinkled at her and Elise frowned. She could swear she turned those off. Remembering how happy she and Jared had been the night before, she concluded they'd forgotten to turn them off and walked to the tree.

"See all the presents for you?" she said, lowering herself and Molly to the floor in front of all the brightly colored wrapped boxes. "Let's see what we have here—"

Seeing two unfamiliar blue packages, she paused. She didn't know when or how Jared had time to buy them presents, but obviously he had. She lifted the first box, saw it was addressed to her, shook it then chastised herself. She could wait until he came into the living room.

She set one of the gifts she had bought Molly on the floor in front of the baby and reached for the camera she'd left on the coffee table the night before so she'd be ready.

"You open that," she coaxed. "Pull on the paper."

As Molly grabbed at the paper, Elise lifted the camera. "Molly, look at Mommy."

"Don't you think that's a few too many things for a baby to do at one time?"

Elise's head snapped up. "Jared?"

Carrying two steaming mugs of coffee he walked into the room. "I thought you wanted me around for Molly's first Christmas?"

She stretched to receive a good morning kiss. "This is going to take a while and I figured you'd find us before she was done."

He set the coffee on the table in front of the sofa and reached beneath the tree for the blue package she'd nearly shaken two seconds before he'd walked in. "Open this."

She took a breath. "Okay." She opened the package, found the box for Dugan's Jewelers and swallowed hard before opening it.

A locket in the shape of a heart.

Tears sprang to her eyes. "You're giving me your heart?"

He nodded. "Even better, I bought it before I left."

She smiled. "That *is* even better."

He pulled his hand from behind his back and produced a diamond engagement ring.

She stared at it, then at him. "Where'd— How'd you get that?"

He laughed. "Let's just say Mr. Dugan and I were up very early this morning. So, what do you say? Gonna let me make an honest woman of you?"

She laughed and sprang from the floor, throwing herself into his arms. "Yes."

And finally it was the perfect Christmas.

MILLS & BOON®
Pure reading pleasure™

OCTOBER 2008 HARDBACK TITLES

ROMANCE

The Greek Tycoon's Disobedient Bride   978 0 263 20366 0
Lynne Graham

The Venetian's Midnight Mistress   978 0 263 20367 7
Carole Mortimer

Ruthless Tycoon, Innocent Wife *Helen Brooks*   978 0 263 20368 4

The Sheikh's Wayward Wife *Sandra Marton*   978 0 263 20369 1

The Fiorenza Forced Marriage *Melanie Milburne* 978 0 263 20370 7

The Spanish Billionaire's Christmas Bride   978 0 263 20371 4
Maggie Cox

The Ruthless Italian's Inexperienced Wife   978 0 263 20372 1
Christina Hollis

Claimed for the Italian's Revenge *Natalie Rivers* 978 0 263 20373 8

The Italian's Christmas Miracle *Lucy Gordon*   978 0 263 20374 5

Cinderella and the Cowboy *Judy Christenberry*   978 0 263 20375 2

His Mistletoe Bride *Cara Colter*   978 0 263 20376 9

Pregnant: Father Wanted *Claire Baxter*   978 0 263 20377 6

Marry-Me Christmas *Shirley Jump*   978 0 263 20378 3

Her Baby's First Christmas *Susan Meier*   978 0 263 20379 0

One Magical Christmas *Carol Marinelli*   978 0 263 20380 6

The GP's Meant-To-Be Bride *Jennifer Taylor*   978 0 263 20381 3

HISTORICAL

Miss Winbolt and the Fortune Hunter   978 0 263 20213 7
Sylvia Andrew

Captain Fawley's Innocent Bride *Annie Burrows*   978 0 263 20214 4

The Rake's Rebellious Lady *Anne Herries*   978 0 263 20215 1

MEDICAL™

A Mummy for Christmas *Caroline Anderson*   978 0 263 19914 7

A Bride and Child Worth Waiting For   978 0 263 19915 4
Marion Lennox

The Italian Surgeon's Christmas Miracle   978 0 263 19916 1
Alison Roberts

Children's Doctor, Christmas Bride *Lucy Clark*   978 0 263 19917 8

MILLS & BOON®
Pure reading pleasure™

OCTOBER 2008 LARGE PRINT TITLES

ROMANCE

The Sheikh's Blackmailed Mistress *Penny Jordan*	978 0 263 20082 9
The Millionaire's Inexperienced Love-Slave *Miranda Lee*	978 0 263 20083 6
Bought: The Greek's Innocent Virgin *Sarah Morgan*	978 0 263 20084 3
Bedded at the Billionaire's Convenience *Cathy Williams*	978 0 263 20085 0
The Pregnancy Promise *Barbara McMahon*	978 0 263 20086 7
The Italian's Cinderella Bride *Lucy Gordon*	978 0 263 20087 4
Saying Yes to the Millionaire *Fiona Harper*	978 0 263 20088 1
Her Royal Wedding Wish *Cara Colter*	978 0 263 20089 8

HISTORICAL

Untouched Mistress *Margaret McPhee*	978 0 263 20169 7
A Less Than Perfect Lady *Elizabeth Beacon*	978 0 263 20170 3
Viking Warrior, Unwilling Wife *Michelle Styles*	978 0 263 20171 0

MEDICAL™

The Doctor's Royal Love-Child *Kate Hardy*	978 0 263 19980 2
His Island Bride *Marion Lennox*	978 0 263 19981 9
A Consultant Beyond Compare *Joanna Neil*	978 0 263 19982 6
The Surgeon Boss's Bride *Melanie Milburne*	978 0 263 19983 3
A Wife Worth Waiting For *Maggie Kingsley*	978 0 263 19984 0
Desert Prince, Expectant Mother *Olivia Gates*	978 0 263 19985 7

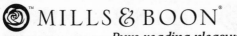

MILLS & BOON®
Pure reading pleasure™

NOVEMBER 2008 HARDBACK TITLES

ROMANCE

The Billionaire's Bride of Vengeance *Miranda Lee*	978 0 263 20382 0
The Santangeli Marriage *Sara Craven*	978 0 263 20383 7
The Spaniard's Virgin Housekeeper *Diana Hamilton*	978 0 263 20384 4
The Greek Tycoon's Reluctant Bride *Kate Hewitt*	978 0 263 20385 1
Innocent Mistress, Royal Wife *Robyn Donald*	978 0 263 20386 8
Taken for Revenge, Bedded for Pleasure *India Grey*	978 0 263 20387 5
The Billionaire Boss's Innocent Bride *Lindsay Armstrong*	978 0 263 20388 2
The Billionaire's Defiant Wife *Amanda Browning*	978 0 263 20389 9
Nanny to the Billionaire's Son *Barbara McMahon*	978 0 263 20390 5
Cinderella and the Sheikh *Natasha Oakley*	978 0 263 20391 2
Promoted: Secretary to Bride! *Jennie Adams*	978 0 263 20392 9
The Black Sheep's Proposal *Patricia Thayer*	978 0 263 20393 6
The Snow-Kissed Bride *Linda Goodnight*	978 0 263 20394 3
The Rancher's Runaway Princess *Donna Alward*	978 0 263 20395 0
The Greek Doctor's New-Year Baby *Kate Hardy*	978 0 263 20396 7
The Wife He's Been Waiting For *Dianne Drake*	978 0 263 20397 4

HISTORICAL

The Captain's Forbidden Miss *Margaret McPhee*	978 0 263 20216 8
The Earl and the Hoyden *Mary Nichols*	978 0 263 20217 5
From Governess to Society Bride *Helen Dickson*	978 0 263 20218 2

MEDICAL™

The Heart Surgeon's Secret Child *Meredith Webber*	978 0 263 19918 5
The Midwife's Little Miracle *Fiona McArthur*	978 0 263 19919 2
The Single Dad's New-Year Bride *Amy Andrews*	978 0 263 19920 8
Posh Doc Claims His Bride *Anne Fraser*	978 0 263 19921 5

MILLS & BOON®
Pure reading pleasure™

NOVEMBER 2008 LARGE PRINT TITLES

ROMANCE

Bought for Revenge, Bedded for Pleasure *Emma Darcy*	978 0 263 20090 4
Forbidden: The Billionaire's Virgin Princess *Lucy Monroe*	978 0 263 20091 1
The Greek Tycoon's Convenient Wife *Sharon Kendrick*	978 0 263 20092 8
The Marciano Love-Child *Melanie Milburne*	978 0 263 20093 5
Parents in Training *Barbara McMahon*	978 0 263 20094 2
Newlyweds of Convenience *Jessica Hart*	978 0 263 20095 9
The Desert Prince's Proposal *Nicola Marsh*	978 0 263 20096 6
Adopted: Outback Baby *Barbara Hannay*	978 0 263 20097 3

HISTORICAL

The Virtuous Courtesan *Mary Brendan*	978 0 263 20172 7
The Homeless Heiress *Anne Herries*	978 0 263 20173 4
Rebel Lady, Convenient Wife *June Francis*	978 0 263 20174 1

MEDICAL™

Nurse Bride, Bayside Wedding *Gill Sanderson*	978 0 263 19986 4
Billionaire Doctor, Ordinary Nurse *Carol Marinelli*	978 0 263 19987 1
The Sheikh Surgeon's Baby *Meredith Webber*	978 0 263 19988 8
The Outback Doctor's Surprise Bride *Amy Andrews*	978 0 263 19989 5
A Wedding at Limestone Coast *Lucy Clark*	978 0 263 19990 1
The Doctor's Meant-To-Be Marriage *Janice Lynn*	978 0 263 19991 8